Fugue for a D...

Also by Christopher Priest from Gollancz:

Inverted World
The Affirmation
The Glamour
The Prestige
The Extremes
The Separation
The Dream Archipelago

Fugue for a Darkening Island

·

Christopher Priest

First published in Great Britain in 1972 by
Faber and Faber

This edition published in Great Britain in 2011 by
Gollancz
An imprint of the Orion Publishing Group
Orion House, 5 Upper St Martin's Lane,
London WC2H 9EA
An Hachette UK Company

1 3 5 7 9 10 8 6 4 2

A CIP catalogue record for this book
is available from the British Library

ISBN 978 0 575 09820 6

Typeset by Deltatype Ltd, Birkenhead, Merseyside

Printed and bound in the UK by
CPI Mackays, Chatham, Kent

The Orion Publishing Group's policy is to use papers
that are natural, renewable and recyclable products and
made from wood grown in sustainable forests. The logging
and manufacturing processes are expected to conform to
the environmental regulations of the country of origin.

www.christopher-priest.co.uk
www.orionbooks.co.uk

FOREWORD

•

I wrote *Fugue for a Darkening Island* in 1971 and it was published in hardcover the following year. Although it is not a political story, it is about the *effects* of politics and that sort of subject was certainly an influence at the time of writing. The main instinct behind it, though, was a literary one.

I was a young and newly established freelance writer and I was still feeling my way, basically trying to decide whether or not I wanted to write science fiction. One of the traditions of British science fiction is the 'disaster' or 'catastrophe' novel, popular during the 1950s. Authors like John Wyndham, John Christopher, Charles Eric Maine, J. T. McIntosh (and a few others) came up with many ingenious ways of ending the world, and are now identified with the form. In 1971, I was reflecting that it had been several years since anyone had tried to write a disaster novel of that kind, and I wondered if it would still be possible in what then felt like the modern age.

The 1950s period for those earlier books was not coincidental. This was the aftermath of the Second World War, in which the country was going through a difficult period, with a wrecked economy, many cities in ruins, food and power in short supply. In addition there was the background thunder of an Empire collapsing. Several writers and critics have observed that while novels like *The Day of the Triffids* (Wyndham) or *The World in Winter* (Christopher) were being written, both their authors and their readers were living in a country where foreground and background were uniquely depressing.

That was not the case when I was contemplating *Fugue* at the beginning of the 1970s. Britain had become a prosperous, exciting and creative place again. Depressing thoughts were far away. On the face of it my idea of writing an updated version of the form seemed rather abstract, like a workshop exercise.

Perhaps others were thinking along the same lines. The July 1968 edition of the magazine *New Worlds* carried a cover by the American film-maker Steve Dwoskin. His graphic consisted of eight plain words: *What is the exact nature of the catastrophe?* I've no idea what Dwoskin intended by this, but the rhetorical question actually spoke to me. It made me wonder, in the context of disaster novels, what truly was the nature of the catastrophe being described. Such novels all dealt with a series of external events which led to a breakdown of civilization around the world, but in any disaster the only thing that really matters is the impact it has on the people involved.

I started thinking about that approach, to concentrate on the personal impact on one ordinary victim, rather than attempt a picture of global disaster.

But I also required a global disaster.

Although 1971 was a relatively stable period in Britain, there were two great social upheavals in progress, well remembered by those who were there.

The first was the sectarian violence erupting throughout Northern Ireland. This was the background to daily life for everyone in Britain, constantly on television and in the newspapers, with the horrors not only escalating week by week but seeming to add up to an insoluble dilemma. As I had no vested interest in the various sectarian causes, what affected me most was a horrified awareness of so much violence and disruption. Many people were forced to leave their homes, streets were blockaded, paramilitary groups emerged, large sections of the police were not neutral, there was endless cruelty and fighting and rioting, both sides attacked each other with car bombs, guns, punishment beatings and a lot more.

Much of what I went on to describe in *Fugue for a Darkening Island* was my nightmare vision of this sort of violent instability spreading to the rest of the country. It still lacked a global dimension, though, something that might conceivably start it happening.

In 1971, the United Kingdom was being run by the Conservatives, led by Edward Heath. In Africa a problem was arising. For several decades people from the Indian subcontinent had been moving to East African countries, where jobs were available. These people were of uncertain nationhood: although ethnically from India and Pakistan they carried British passports. In the early 1970s, they were suddenly forced by dictatorship régimes to leave Kenya and Uganda and most of them moved to Britain.

Because they numbered in the tens of thousands, agitators from the extreme right wing attempted to stir up racist feelings against the new arrivals. In particular, Enoch Powell, then a member of the government, made several inflammatory speeches, warning, for instance, of 'rivers of blood'. It was a nasty episode, but it was relatively short-lived. Assimilation soon began, and by now is complete.

When I thought about a similar refugee crisis erupting from across the whole of the African continent, I realized

I had a disaster whose global proportions would create the kind of scenario of violence and disruption that I was trying to imagine.

This version of *Fugue for a Darkening Island* is fully revised. I have wanted a chance to modify the book for many years, for a number of reasons.

The main one was that as time went by sensibilities about the subject matter began to change, attitudes to it changed, even the vocabulary of it changed. The story, which I saw as an attempt to describe a global disaster in the ironic and liberal terms of its day, gradually became misunderstood.

This change was for me dramatized by two reviews that were published several years apart in the same magazine: the trendily political *Time Out*.

When *Fugue* was first published the reviewer in *Time Out* was extravagant in his praise. What he saw as my anti-racist views and descriptions of a country torn apart by extremists were highly recommended. A few years later, when the book was republished, *Time Out* reviewed it again. (Different reviewer, but same general political credo.) This time I was criticized for being an agitator, a fellow-traveller of the right wing.

As my novel was politically neutral I felt both critical opinions were off the mark, but I did not like being lined up with racists. It was around that time that I decided I should have to look at the novel again one day. Now it has been done. While I dislike political correctness, I have removed anything that I think could lead to overt political interpretation, on either side.

There was another reason too. *Fugue* was my first attempt at a serious novel, with serious subject matter. It was ambitious and complex and for a while I struggled with the writing of it. For me it was a time when my writing was changing and I was open to influences. Cool detachment was a sort of common literary language at the time and I found it attractive. I had been reading not only the 'new wave' of science fiction writers but also American writers like Richard Brautigan, Kurt Vonnegut Jr and Jerzy Kosinski. I liked their attitude, which allowed for the description of thrilling or horrific events in unemotional language. This seemed to me to heighten the thrills, make the horror more terrible.

But nearly four decades later I'm not so sure that that level of detachment was right for *Fugue*. Some dispassion remains, but this revised version is much more engaged, the weaknesses of the characters are fully acknowledged, the pain hurts more, the anger finds a voice.

It is still the same story as before, but now I believe it works more effectively. It has not been 'up-dated'. For all its depiction of unpleasant events the story was written before the onset of world terrorism. The social and political changes that have taken place because of that are not shown. In this sense *Fugue* is a glimpse of the past. It is also a reminder of a world where there were no emails, no DVDs, no internet, no CCTV cameras, no DNA testing, no mobile phones, no genetically modified food, no digital cameras, no laser or keyhole or stem-cell surgery, no satellite television, Britain had not yet joined the EU, the euro had not been invented ... the list goes on. How the presence of any of these might have affected the way the story was told can now be only a matter for speculation.

Christopher Priest

Fugue for a
Darkening Island

•

I have white skin. Light brown hair. Blue eyes. I am tall. I usually dress conservatively: sports jackets, corduroy trousers, knitted ties. I wear spectacles for reading, though they are more an affectation than a necessity. I smoke cigarettes occasionally. Sometimes I drink alcohol. I do not believe in God; I do not go to church; I do not have any objections to other people doing so. When I married my wife, I was in love with her. I am very fond of my daughter Sally. I have no political ambitions. My name is Alan Whitman.

My skin is smudged with dirt. My hair is dry, salt-encrusted and itchy. I have blue eyes. I am tall. I am wearing now what I was wearing six months ago, and I smell awful. I have lost my spectacles, and learned to live without them. I do not smoke at all most of the time, though when cigarettes are available I smoke them continually. I am able to get drunk about once a month. I do not believe in God; I do not go to church. When I last saw my wife, I was cursing her, though I have learned to regret it. I am very fond of my daughter Sally. I do not think I have political ambitions. My name is Alan Whitman.

*

I met Rafiq in a village ruined by an artillery bombardment. I disliked him the moment I saw him and it was clearly returned. We ignored each other after the first moments of caution. I was looking for food in the village, knowing that as the bombardment was only just over it would not yet have been completely plundered. There were several houses still intact and I ignored these, knowing from experience that the ground troops ransacked these first. It was more fruitful to sift through the rubble of partially destroyed buildings.

Working methodically, by midday I had filled two haversacks with canned food and had stolen for future barter three road maps from abandoned cars. I did not see the other man, Rafiq, again during the morning.

I found a field on the outskirts of the village which had been cultivated at one time. In one corner I discovered a row of freshly dug graves, each marked with a simple piece of wood upon which were stapled metal dog-tags bearing the name of the soldier. I looked at the names, and guessed they had been Africans.

As that part of the field was the most secluded I sat down near the graves and opened one of the cans. The meat stew inside was horrible: half-cooked and greasy. I ate it hungrily.

Afterwards, I walked out to the wreck of the helicopter that had crashed nearby. It was not likely to have any food on board, though if the instruments were recoverable they might be suitable for future exchanges. I needed a compass most of all, though it was unlikely the helicopter would have carried one that could either be easily detached or would be usable without the helicopter power supply. When I reached the wreck I saw that the other man was inside the smashed cockpit, working at the dashboard with a long-bladed knife in an attempt to remove an instrument. When he became aware of my presence he straightened slowly, his hand moving towards a pocket. He turned to face me, and for several minutes we regarded each other carefully, each seeing in the other a man who responded to a situation in the same way as himself.

This was how I fell in with Rafiq and his group.

We realized we would probably be forced to abandon our house in Southgate the day the barricade was erected at the end of our road. Although terrified by the prospect we did nothing, because for several days we thought we might be able to adjust to the new mode of life.

I had no idea who had built the barricade. As we lived at the far end of the road, near to the edge of the playing fields, we did not hear the noises in the night, but when Isobel took the car down the road to take Sally to school she returned almost at once with the news.

It was the first tangible sign in our lives that irrevocable change was taking place in the country. Ours was not the first of such barricades, but there were few others in our particular neighbourhood.

When Isobel told me about it I walked down to see it for myself. It did not appear to be very strongly constructed. It was made mostly of wooden supports and barbed-wire loops, but its symbolism was unmistakable. There were a few men standing around, some of whom I recognized as neighbours. I nodded cautiously to them.

The following day we were at home when we heard the noise of the Martins being evicted. They lived almost opposite us. We had not had much to do with them and since the Afrim landings had seen even less of them. Vincent Martin was a highly qualified research technician and worked at an aircraft components factory in Hatfield. His wife stayed at

3

home, looking after their three children. They were West Indians.

At the time of their eviction I had nothing to do with the street patrol which was responsible for it. Within a week, though, all men in the street had been enrolled, and every member of their families was given a pass which had to be carried at all times as identification. We saw the passes as potentially the most valuable possessions we had, as by this time we were no longer blind to what was going on around us.

Cars were allowed in and out of the street only at certain times and the barricade patrols enforced this rule with absolute inflexibility. As the street opened on to a main road which government regulations kept clear of parked traffic after six in the evening, it meant that if you arrived home after the barricade had closed you had to find somewhere else to park. As most streets quickly followed our example and closed their entrances, this meant that you had to leave your car at a great distance from home, and walking the rest of the way at such a time was hazardous.

The normal strength of a street patrol was two men, although on a few occasions this was doubled and on the night before we finally decided to leave there were fourteen men. I was part of a patrol three times; sharing the duty with a different man each time. Our function was simple. While one man stayed at the barricade with the shotgun, the other walked up and down the street four times. The positions were then reversed, and so on through the night.

While I was at the barricade I was always most worried in case a police car came along. Although I did see their cars on many occasions, none of them ever stopped. During meetings of the patrol committee, the question of what to do in

4

such an event was often raised but no satisfactory answer was given, at least as far as I was concerned.

In practice we and the police would leave each other alone, though everyone heard stories of battles between the occupants of barricaded streets and riot-shielded police. No news of these fights ever appeared in the newspapers or on television, and the absence was more noticeable than the news itself would have been.

The true purpose of the shotgun was to deter illegal squatters from attempting to enter the street, and secondarily to show it as a form of protest. If the government and the armed forces were unable or unwilling to protect our homes then we would take the matter into our own hands. Such was the essence of what was printed on the backs of our pass tickets, and was the unspoken creed of the men on the street patrol. We had literally taken the law into our own hands.

For my own part I was uneasy. The burnt-out shell of the Martins' house opposite ours was a constant reminder of the violence inherent in the patrols, and the never-ending parade of homeless shambling through the night past the barricades was upsetting.

I was asleep at home during the night the barricade on the next street fell. I had heard that the patrol was to be enlarged because of the way things were going, but it was not my turn of duty.

Our first awareness of the fighting in the next street was the firing of a shot nearby. While Isobel took Sally downstairs to shelter in the space beneath the staircase, I dressed hurriedly and went to join the patrol at the barricade. Here, the men of the street stared sullenly at the army lorries and police vans parked across the main road. About thirty armed soldiers faced us, obviously nervous of what we might do, or even perhaps of what they might be ordered to do.

Three water cannons rumbled past and disappeared through the jumble of military vehicles towards the next street. From time to time we heard more shots and the sound of voices shouting angrily. A few of the explosions were deeper and more powerful and slowly a red glow brightened, silhouetting the houses that were opposite the end of our gardens. More army lorries and police vans arrived and the men inside ran towards the street. We at our barricade said nothing, only too aware of the flagrant provocation and absolute inadequacy that our solitary shotgun represented. It was kept fully loaded, but out of sight. At that time, I would not have liked to be the man holding it.

We waited at the barricade all night, listening to the sounds of the battle only a short distance away. As dawn came the noise gradually lessened. We saw the bodies of several soldiers and policemen carried away, and many more wounded were driven off in ambulances.

As the full light of day arrived, nearly two hundred white people, some dressed in only their nightclothes, were escorted by the police towards a fleet of ambulances and lorries parked by the Underground station at the far end of the main road. As they passed our barricade some of them tried to argue or reason with us, pleading to be taken in, but were herded on by the soldiers. While they passed I looked at the men on our side of the barricade and wondered whether the hard lack of expression was also on my own face.

We waited for the activity outside to die down, but the sound of gunfire continued sporadically for many hours. We saw no normal traffic on the road and assumed that it had been diverted. One of the men at our barricade was carrying a transistor radio, and we listened anxiously to each of the BBC's news bulletins hoping to hear some word of reassurance.

By ten o'clock in the morning it was apparent that events were quietening down. Most of the police vehicles had driven away but the army was still around us. About once every five minutes there was a gunshot, but the firing was some distance away. A few houses in the next street were still burning but there was no sign of the fires spreading.

As soon as I could manage it I slipped away from the barricade and walked back to my house.

I found Isobel and Sally still sheltering under the stairs. Isobel had withdrawn almost entirely into her fear. She had lost all colour in her face, the pupils of her eyes were dilated and she slurred her speech when she spoke. Sally was little better. Their story was a garbled and incomplete recounting of a series of events they had experienced at second hand: explosions, shouting voices, gunfire and the spreading crackle of burning wood, all heard as they huddled in a terrified state in the dark. While I made them tea and warmed up some food, I inspected the damage to the house.

A petrol bomb had exploded in the garden, setting fire to our shed. All the windows at the back of the house had been broken or cracked, and I found several bullets lodged in the walls. Even as I stood in the back room a bullet flew through the window and narrowly missed me.

I crawled on my hands and knees to the window and peered through.

Our house normally had a view across the gardens to the houses in the next street. As I knelt there I saw that of them only about a half of those buildings were still intact. I could see movement through the windows of some of these, as people passed through the rooms. One man, a short guy in filthy clothes, stood in the garden sheltering behind a part of a fence. It was he who had fired his gun at me. As I watched he fired again, this time at the house next to mine.

7

When Isobel and Sally were dressed we took the three suitcases we had packed the previous week and I put them in the car. While Isobel went through the house and systematically locked all interconnecting doors and cupboards, I collected our cash.

Shortly afterwards, we drove down to the barricade. Here we were stopped by the other men.

'Where do you think you're going, Whitman?' one of them asked me. It was Johnson, one of the men with whom I had shared a patrol three nights before.

'We're leaving,' I said. 'We're going to Isobel's parents.'

Johnson reached in through the open window, turned off the ignition before I could stop him. He withdrew the key.

'Sorry,' he said. 'No one leaves. If we all ran out, these people would swarm in like vermin.'

Several of the men had crowded round. By my side, I felt Isobel tense. Sally was in the back. I didn't care to think how this was affecting her.

'We can't stay here. Our house overlooks those others. It's only a matter of time before they come through the gardens.'

I saw several of the men glance at one another.

Johnson, whose house was not on the same side as ours, said stubbornly, 'We have to stick together. It's our only hope.'

Isobel leaned over me and looked up at Johnson imploringly.

'Please,' she said. 'Have you thought of us? What about your own wife? Does she want to stay?'

'It's only a matter of time,' I said again. 'You've seen what has happened in other places. Once the Afrims have a street to themselves, they spread through the rest of the district in a few nights.'

'But the law is on our side,' one of the other men said, nodding his head in the direction of the soldiers outside the barricade.

'They're not on anyone's side. You might as well pull down the barricade. It's useless now.'

Johnson moved away from the car window and went to speak to one of the other men. It was Nicholson, one of the leaders of the patrol committee. After a few seconds, Nicholson himself came over.

'You're not leaving,' he said finally. 'No one's leaving. Get the car away from here and come back on barricade duty. It's all we can do.'

He tossed in the ignition key and it fell on Isobel's lap. She picked it up. I wound the handle and closed the window tightly.

As I started the engine, I said to Isobel, 'Do you want to chance it?'

She looked at the men in front of us and at the barbed wire barricade, then at the armed soldiers beyond it. She said nothing.

Behind us, Sally was crying.

'I want to go home, Daddy,' she said.

I turned the car round and drove back slowly to our house. As we passed one of the other houses on the same side of the street as our own, we heard the sound of a woman screaming inside. I glanced at Isobel and saw her close her eyes.

I stopped the car by the house. It looked so normal, so familiar. We sat in the car and made no move to get out. I left the engine running. To turn it off would have been too final.

After a while I put the car into forward gear and drove down to the end of the street, towards the recreation field. When the barricade had been erected at the main road end, only two strands of wire had been put across here and it was normally unmanned. So it was now. There was no one around. Like the rest of the street the appearance of the sports field was at once disturbingly normal and abnormal. I stopped the car, jumped out and pulled down the wire. Beyond it was a wooden fence held in place by a row of stakes. I tried it with my hands, and found that it was firm but not immovable.

I drove the car over the wire and stopped with the bumper touching the wooden fence. In first gear I pushed the fence until it snapped and fell. In front of us the recreation field was deserted.

I drove across it, feeling the car lurch in and out of the ruts of the previous year's sport.

I pulled myself out of the water and lay on the bank of the river, struggling to recover my breath. The physical shock of the cold water had exhausted me. Every part of my body ached and throbbed. I lay still, trying to will the warmth back into my body.

Five minutes later I stood up then looked back across the water to where Isobel and Sally were waiting for me. I walked upstream until I was directly opposite them, carrying the end of the rope I had towed behind me. Isobel was sitting on the soil of the bank, not watching me but staring blankly downstream. By her side Sally stood attentively.

I shouted instructions to them across the water. I saw Sally saying something to Isobel, and Isobel shaking her head. I stood impatiently, feeling my muscles shivering into the beginnings of cramp. I shouted again and Isobel stood up. Sally and she tied the end of the rope around their waists and across their chests in the manner I had shown them, then walked nervously to the edge of the water.

10

In my impatience I may have pulled the rope too hard. Just as they reached the edge of the water they fell forward and began floundering in the shallows. Isobel could not swim and was afraid of drowning. I could see Sally struggling with her, trying to prevent her mother from crawling back to the bank.

Taking the initiative from both of them I pulled the rope as hard as I could, towing them out into the centre of the river. Whenever Isobel's face came above the surface, she shouted and screamed in a mixture of fear and anger.

In just under a minute I had them on my side. Sally lay on the muddy bank, staring at me silently. I wanted her to criticize me for what I had done, but she said nothing. Isobel lay on her side, doubled over. She was coughing and choking, spitting out water. When she could speak, her first words were to swear at me. I ignored her.

Although the river was cold from the hills the air was warm. We took stock of our possessions. Nothing had been lost in the crossing, but everything we carried had become soaked. It had been part of the original plan that Isobel should hold our main haversack up out of the water, while Sally supported her. Now all our clothes and food were wet, and our matches for lighting a fire were unusable. We decided it would be best if we removed all our clothes. We took off the outer garments and hung them in the bushes and trees in the hope that they would be dry enough to wear by morning.

We lay together on the ground, shivering miserably, and cuddling each other for warmth. Within half an hour Isobel was asleep, but Sally lay in my arms with her eyes open.

We each knew the other was awake and stayed so for most of the night.

*

I was to spend the night with a woman named Louise. She had booked a room in a hotel in Goodge Street, and as I had told Isobel that I was taking part in a midnight demonstration at the college I was able to get away from home for a whole night.

Louise and I dined at a small Greek restaurant in Charlotte Street, then, not wishing to spend the entire evening in her hotel room, we went to a cinema in Tottenham Court Road. I cannot recall the title of the film. All I can remember is that it was foreign, that its dialogue was subtitled in English and that it concerned a violently resolved love affair between a coloured man and a white woman. The film contained several scenes of complete sexual frankness. Although the film had not been formally banned, few cinemas were willing to show it. Other cinemas showing films with explicit scenes of the physical act of love had been raided by the police. At the time we saw this film it had been showing for more than a year without any intervention from the authorities.

However, we were unlucky with the date and we made the wrong choice of film. We had bought seats at the rear of the cinema, so when the police burst in by way of the emergency exit doors along each side of the auditorium we were able to see the worked out strategy of the raid. Care had obviously gone into it, ensuring not only surprise but that no one should be able to leave the theatre without being identified and questioned. An armed officer stood at each door and a dozen others formed a cordon around the audience.

For a minute or two there seemed to be no further action. The film continued to play until the house lights went up, and even then went on being shown for several more minutes, its pornographic coupling a dim but alluring image on the screen. When finally it stopped, it did so suddenly, with a series of noisy electronic clicks on the loudspeakers.

We sat in the auditorium for twenty minutes without knowing what was going to happen to us. One of the policemen forming part of the cordon was near me and I asked him what was going on. He made no answer.

We were ordered to leave the auditorium row by row and to divulge our names and addresses. By chance I was not carrying any form of identification, so I took a risk and gave the police an invented name and address. Although they searched my pockets in an attempt to find confirmation, and they threatened me with arrest for breach of the recently introduced identification law, I was allowed to go free after Louise vouched for my false identity.

We returned to her hotel immediately and went to bed. After the events of the evening I was angry, depressed and frightened. In spite of Louise's best efforts to arouse me, and even though I had been eagerly anticipating this night with her for several days, I was unable to perform. Memories of the fading image of filmed intercourse haunted me.

The UK Reform government, led by the renegade Conservative John Tregarth, had been in power for three months.

Louise was later arrested on a charge of attempting to pervert the course of justice, but because the police were still unable to trace me they eventually released her.

As adversaries we detested the Afrim troops. We continually heard rumours of their cowardice in battle, and of their arrogance in victory, however small or relative it may be.

One day we encountered a member of the Royal Nationalist Air Force who had been captured by an Afrim patrol. This man, who had been a pilot until crippled by the Africans' torture, told us of brutalities and atrocities in their military interrogation centres that made our own experiences as civilians appear to be trivial and perfunctory. The pilot had lost a leg below the knee, and had suffered lacerated tendons in the other. He counted himself as among the more fortunate. He asked us for assistance.

We were reluctant to become involved and Rafiq called a meeting to decide what to do. In the end we voted to transport the crippled man to within sight of the RNAF station, and to allow him to find his own way from there.

Shortly after this incident we were rounded up by an Afrim patrol and taken to one of their civilian interrogation centres.

We said nothing to them about the pilot, nor about Afrim tactics in general. On this occasion we made no attempt to resist arrest. I was in a passive state after the recent abduction of the women and I could not get out of my mind the idea that we were being targeted. I was weary and depressed, and had no strength for any kind of resistance, even token resistance. As for the rest of the group, maybe they felt the same way. Certainly, since the women had been taken we were all in a lethargic state.

We were driven in a small convoy to a building on the outskirts of one of the Afrim-held towns. In a large marquee in the grounds we were ordered to strip and pass through a delousing section. This was a part of the tent which had been partitioned off and filled with a dense steam. Coming out a few minutes later, we were told to dress again. Our clothes lay untouched where we had left them.

We were then divided into groups of one, two or three men. I was one of those on my own. We were taken to rooms inside the main building and interrogated briefly. My own interrogator was a tall West African, who, in spite of the central-heating system, wore a brown greatcoat. I had noticed on entering the room that the two uniformed guards in the corridor had been holding Russian rifles.

The interrogation was sketchy. Identification papers, certificate of state and origin and Afrim-stamped photograph were all shown and checked.

'Your destination, Mr Whitman?'

'Dorchester,' I said, giving him the answer we had agreed upon in the event of arrest.

'You have relatives there?'

'Yes.' I gave him the name and address of fictitious parents.

'You have a family?'

'Yes.'

'But they are not with you.'

'No.'

'Who is the leader of your group?'

'We don't have a leader.'

There was a long silence while he scrutinized my papers again. After this I was returned to the marquee where I waited with the others as the rest of the interrogations were completed. Then two Afrims in civilian clothes went through our possessions. The search was superficial, turning up only a fork for eating that one of the men had left near the top of his haversack. The two knives I had secreted in the lining of my own bag went undetected.

After this search there was another long period of waiting, until a lorry bearing a large red cross on a white background was driven up alongside the marquee. The agreed Red Cross humanitarian supply to refugees had been set for some time at one and a half kilos of protein a week, but since the Afrims had been handling their own side of the arrangement, the quantity had decreased steadily. I received two small cans of processed meat and a packet of forty cigarettes.

Later, we were driven away from the town in three lorries and dumped in the countryside a long way from where we had been arrested. It took us the whole of the next day and part of the day following to locate our supplies. We had cached them hurriedly as soon as we realized we were about to be arrested.

At no time during our involuntary visit to Afrim-occupied territory had we seen or heard any sign or hint of the women who had been taken from us. That night I lay awake, despairing of seeing Sally and Isobel again.

It was reported on the early news that the unidentified ship which had been sailing up the English Channel for the last two days had entered the Thames estuary.

During the morning I followed the regular bulletins on the radio. The ship refused to stop when challenged and had neither answered nor made any radio signals since first being sighted. It was not flying any flag. It was being shadowed by a Royal Navy minesweeper, but because of the recent UN resolution they could not use force to intercept it. A pilot cutter had gone out to it from Tilbury but the officials were not able to board it. The name on her bows and stern had been painted over, but it was still possible to decipher it. From this, the ship had been identified as a 10,000-tonne cargo tramp, registered in Liberia and according to Lloyd's was most recently chartered to a shipping firm in Lagos. However, because of the chaos all over West Africa, the concept of 'recently' could mean anything between one and ten years ago.

As it happened I was free to leave the college after twelve-thirty, and not having any lectures or tutorials in the afternoon I decided to go down to the river. I caught a bus to Cannon Street and walked out on to London Bridge. Several hundred other people, presumably some of the workers from nearby offices, had had the same idea. The eastern side of the bridge, facing downstream, was crowded.

As time passed several people moved away, apparently to return to their offices. I was slowly able to move forward to the parapet of the bridge.

At just after two-thirty we were able to make out the ship, coming up the river towards Tower Bridge. We saw that there were many craft in attendance around it and amongst them were launches of the river police. A wave of speculation passed through the crowd.

The ship approached the bridge, which kept its road down. A man standing near to me had a small pair of field-glasses and he told us that the pedestrians on the bridge were being moved off. The road was being closed to traffic. A few seconds later the bridge opened just in time for the ship to pass through.

I was aware of sirens close at hand. Turning, I saw that half a dozen police cars had driven on to London Bridge. The men remained inside, but left the blue lights flashing on the roofs. The ship came on steadily towards us.

Soon we could see that several men on the small launches around the ship were attempting to communicate through loudhailers with those on board. We could not make out what was said but the sound came to us across the water in tinny resonances. Because the police had by now sealed off both ends of London Bridge it became unnaturally quiet. Further away from me I saw them trying to move some of the crowd along, but everyone was resisting, pushing back to the bridge parapet so that they could see what was going to happen. In our part of the bridge, a single mounted policeman rode up and down on his huge chestnut mare. He yelled at us to leave the bridge but only a handful of people obeyed.

The ship was now so close it felt as if it would be possible to reach down and touch the superstructure. Everyone could see that its decks were crowded with people, some of whom were lying down. Two of the police launches had reached London Bridge and had turned back to face the oncoming ship. From one of them a policeman with a loudhailer shouted to the captain of the ship to stop his engines and to submit to a boarding party.

There was no acknowledgement from the ship, which sailed on slowly towards the bridge, though many of the people on the decks of the ship were shouting back at the police, unable to make themselves understood.

The bows of the ship passed underneath an arch of the bridge just to one side of where I was standing. I looked down at it. The decks were crowded to the rails with people. Most of them were staring up at us. A few waved their arms but almost everyone was shouting. I had no more time to look at them because the superstructure amidships crashed into the parapet of the bridge. It was a slow, grinding collision, making an ugly scraping noise of metal on stone. I saw that the paintwork of the ship and its superstructure was filthy and rusty, with many panes of broken glass in the ports.

I looked down at the river and saw that the police launches and two river authority tugs had gone in against the hull of the old ship and were trying to push her stern around towards the concrete bank of the New Fresh Wharf. From the thick black smoke still issuing from her funnel, and from the white-cream frothing water at the stern, it was clear that the ship's engines were still running. As the tugs made headway in pushing her towards the bank the metal superstructure scraped and crashed repeatedly against the bridge.

I saw movement on the ship, on the decks and inside. The

people on board were moving towards the stern. Many of them fell as they ran. As the stern rammed into the concrete quay the first men jumped ashore.

The ship was wedged firmly between the bank and the bridge, her bows still under the arch, her superstructure against the parapet and her stern overhanging the quay. A tug moved round to the bridge, to make sure that until the engines were stopped the ship wouldn't turn somehow and move back into the river. Four police launches were now against her port side, and ropes and rope ladders were thrown with grappling irons up towards the decks. The fleeing passengers made no efforts to remove them. When the first ladder was secured the police and customs officials began to climb it.

On London Bridge, all our attention was now on the sight of the people leaving the ship. The African refugees were coming ashore.

We watched them with a mixture of horror and fascination. There were men, women and children. Most if not all were thin and looking unwell, severely malnourished. Skeletal arms and legs, distended stomachs, skull-like heads holding staring eyes; flat, paper-like breasts on the women, accusing faces on them all. Most were naked or nearly so. Many of the children could not walk. Those whom no one would carry were left on the ship.

A metal door in the side of the ship was opened from within and a gangway was pushed across the strip of water to the quay. From below decks more Africans came pouring out on to the shore. Some fell to the concrete as they stepped on the land, others moved towards the wharf building and disappeared either into it or around its sides. None of them looked up at us on the bridge, or back at their fellows who were in the process of leaving the ship.

We waited and watched. There seemed to be no end to the number of people on board.

In time, the upper decks were cleared although people still poured ashore from below. I tried to count the number of people lying, dead or unconscious, on the deck. When I had reached one hundred, I stopped counting.

The men who had gone aboard finally managed to stop the engines and the ship was made fast to the quay. Many ambulances had arrived at the wharf and those people suffering most were put inside and driven away.

But hundreds more just wandered from the wharf, away from the river and up into the streets of the City, whose occupants could know nothing as yet of the events on the river.

I learned later that the police and the river authorities had found more than seven hundred bodies on the ship, most of them children. The welfare authorities accounted for another four and a half thousand survivors, who were taken to hospitals or emergency centres. There was no way of counting the remainder, though I heard once an estimate that at least three thousand people had wandered away from the ship and tried to survive alone. Many of them were rounded up but most of them managed to elude the authorities. They disappeared into the anonymity of the great city.

Shortly after the ship had been secured we were moved off the bridge by the police, who told us that because of the collision with the ship the structure was now unsafe. The following day, however, the bridge was open again to traffic.

The event I had witnessed became known in time as the first of the Afrim landings. There were three more in London before the Thames estuary was secured against intrusion, but most of the refugees arrived in small boats and dinghies, offloaded out at sea from the larger ships. Their occupants landed anywhere they could, on beaches and shingle banks, in tiny ports and alongside the promenades of seaside towns. They waded or swam or stumbled ashore, day and night, week after week, for nearly two years. The African continent had become uninhabitable, and millions of refugees were spreading out around the world.

We were flagged down by a patrolling police car and questioned on the side of the road. They wanted to know where we were going. We were quizzed closely about why we had left our home. Isobel explained about the invasion of the houses in the next street and the imminent danger in which our home had been.

While we waited for permission to continue Sally tried to soothe Isobel, who after rushing out the explanation to the police office was taken by a flood of tears. I did not want to show the same emotion. While sharing her feelings and still trying to grasp the idea that we might really have lost our home, I had been putting up with Isobel's emotional instability for the last few months. It had been understandably awkward while I was working at the cloth factory, the only job I could find, but in comparison with what had happened to some of the other lecturers at the college, we were relatively well off. I made every attempt to be sympathetic and patient with her, but we had succeeded only in reviving our old squabbles.

In a few moments the police officer returned to our car and informed us that we could proceed on condition we headed for the UN camp at Horsenden Hill in Middlesex. Our original destination had been Isobel's parents, who now lived in Bristol.

The policeman told us that civilians should not try to

make long-distance journeys across country after dark. We had spent most of the afternoon cruising about the London suburbs in an attempt to find a garage that would sell us enough petrol to fill not only the tank of the car, but also the three five-gallon cans I carried in the boot. Now it was beginning to get dark and we were almost as far away from Bristol as we had been when we left home. All three of us were hungry.

I drove along the Western Avenue towards Alperton, after having made a wide detour through Kensington, Fulham and Hammersmith to avoid the barricaded Afrim enclaves at Notting Hill and North Kensington. The main road itself was clear of obstructions, although we saw that every side road and one or two of the subsidiary main roads that crossed were barricaded and manned by armed civilians. At Hanger Lane we turned off the Western Avenue and drove up through Alperton, along the route we had been directed. At several points we saw parked police vehicles, several dozen uniformed police and many blue-helmeted UN militiamen.

At the gates of the camp we were again detained and interrogated, but this was only to be expected. In particular, we were questioned about the reasons we had left our home and what precautions had been made to secure it while we were away.

I told them that the street in which we lived had been barricaded, that we had closed and locked every door in the house, for which we had keys, and that troops and police were in the neighbourhood. While I spoke, one of the questioners wrote in a small notebook. We had to give our full address and the names of the men at the barricades. We waited in the car while the information was relayed by telephone. In the end we were told to park the car in a space just inside the gates and to take our belongings on foot to the main reception centre.

The buildings were further from the gates than we had expected, and when we reached them we were surprised to find that they consisted mainly of light prefabricated huts. On the front of one of them was a painted board, written in several different languages, and which was illuminated by a floodlight. It directed us to separate; men to go towards a hut known as D Central, and women and children to enter this one.

I said to Isobel, 'We'll see each other later, I suppose.'

She leaned over and kissed me briefly. I kissed Sally. They went into the hut, leaving me on my own with the suitcase.

I followed the directions and found D Central. Inside, I was told to surrender the suitcase for search, and to take off my clothes. I complied with this reluctantly, and my clothes and suitcase were taken away together. I was then instructed to go through a shower of hot water and to scrub myself clean. Understanding the probable reasoning behind this I complied, even though I had bathed only the night before.

When I came out I was given a towel and some rough clothing. I asked if I could have my own clothes back. This was refused, but I was told that I could have my night clothes later.

When I had dressed I was ushered into a plain hall which was full of men. All races were present, in about equal numbers.

The men were sitting at benches, eating, smoking and talking. I was instructed to take a bowl of food from the serving hatch, and although this did not satisfy my hunger, I was told I might have more if I requested it. At the same time, I learned that cigarettes could be obtained at the hatch and I collected a packet of twenty.

I was wondering about Isobel and Sally and assumed that they were receiving similar treatment somewhere else. I could only hope that we would be reunited before going to bed.

After a couple of hours we were told we should disperse and we were led to some other huts in the compound, where we were to sleep on hard, narrow beds. Each bed had only a single blanket, and there was no pillow. I did not see Isobel and Sally.

In the morning I found the hut where they had been sleeping and we spent an hour together.

They told me how badly they were being treated in the women's quarters and that they had not been able to sleep. While talking about this we heard a radio report that the government had reached a negotiated settlement with the leaders of the militant Afrims and that everything would be back to normal in a matter of days.

It was this that made us decide to return home. It was what we all wanted, and Sally began crying with relief when she realized what it meant. Something about the way the information was announced did make both Isobel and me suspicious that perhaps things weren't as clear-cut as they were saying, but we decided that going home was all we really wanted to do. We agreed we would go there and see how things stood in the neighbourhood. If we had to we could resume our journey to Bristol, or even return to this camp.

After a great deal of difficulty and delays we contacted a UN official in the camp and told him we wished to leave. He seemed reluctant to agree to this, and said that far too many people were trying to return to their homes. He warned us not to believe everything that was said by government spokesmen and that the overall situation was much more complicated than anyone realized. He advised us not to venture out. We told him that we considered our home to be safe after all. He warned us that the camp was nearly full and that if we left now he would not be able to guarantee us a place should we return.

In spite of this, we left the camp after retrieving our clothes and our car. Although our suitcases had obviously been searched, none of our belongings was missing.

At the time of the second Afrim landing I was attending an academic conference in Harrogate. I don't remember much of what went on there during the formal proceedings, because I was not all that interested in the subjects up for discussion. I had volunteered to attend on behalf of my department at the college as a way of taking a break from the emotional tensions at home. Isobel and I were going through another bad patch. I remember, though, that the event was efficiently organized and that the formal programme was adhered to rigidly.

Twice I happened to share a table at lunchtime with a young Liberal Arts lecturer from the University of East Anglia, and we became friendly. Her name was Alexandra. During the second of our lunches we were interrupted by the arrival of someone I knew, an acquaintance from my days at university. We exchanged greetings and he joined us at the table. I did not actually remember much about him, except that he and I had never been close friends, and I was not particularly pleased to see him. We chatted, though. Soon after he arrived, Alexandra picked up her plate and tray and moved to another table.

My thoughts turned to Alexandra during the afternoon,

wondering if I had somehow offended her, or perhaps it was the other man she didn't want to be around. I made several attempts to locate her, without success. She did not appear for dinner and in the end I assumed she had gone home early.

After dinner I went to the bar with some of the others but once we were there I didn't feel like company. I went for a walk around the town centre, then returned to the hotel.

A little later, as I was sitting on the end of my bed in my hotel room, idly watching TV, there was a knock at my door. It was Alexandra. She came in, brandishing a half-bottle of Scotch. We drank together, while she told me a series of stories about her past relationship with the chap who had interrupted our lunch. She was fun to listen to, and easy to talk to.

Later, we made love together on my bed, and she stayed in my room for the rest of the night.

The following day was the end of the conference, and apart from a small ceremony in the main hall there were to be no formal events. Alexandra and I shared a table for breakfast. I assumed this was probably the last time we would be together, because neither of us spoke about plans for another meeting. She was wearing a gold band on her third finger, left hand. I was already feeling guilty about her, but I did like her so much. It was during breakfast that we heard about the second Afrim landing near Gravesend, on the Thames estuary, and we talked for several minutes about the significance of the upheavals that would inevitably follow.

Before we parted we spent half an hour alone together, walking through the gardens of the hotel. It was just an interlude for us both. Soon we parted, making our separate ways home.

Following a confused discussion with Rafiq, I found myself foraging alone in a deserted town on the south coast. Rafiq had clearly not formed any plan, and his decision to send out several of us searching around for whatever we thought might come in handy to our group was impulsive and irrational. My task was as ill-defined as his instructions. When Rafiq lost his temper he became illogical and his speech was difficult to follow. As far as I knew he had decided we should have something with which to defend ourselves, but I had little or no idea where to start. I was apprehensive about what might happen, as this strip of the coast was within Afrim-held territory. The men in their rapidly expanding guerrilla army rarely showed themselves in daylight, but as I moved around I felt my movements were being observed by hidden watchers.

I came to a short parade of shops overlooking the road that ran alongside the shingly beach. Every one of them had been looted. The shops were a desolate line of ruin, their racks emptied by repeated pillaging. In one store I discovered a domestic-sized glass-cutting instrument, which earlier looters must somehow have missed, and pocketed it in the absence of there being anything else of worth.

I moved on down to the shore.

There was a group of white refugees here, living in a crude encampment of old beach huts and tents. Although I approached them with an attempt at a friendly wave they shouted at me to go away. I walked along what had once been the beach promenade in a westerly direction until I was out of their sight.

I came to a long row of bungalows which, to judge by their affluent appearance, at one time would have been occupied by the wealthy retired. I wondered if the Africans had any plans to use them and why the refugees I had seen were not camping there. Most of the bungalows were unlocked and there appeared to be nothing to prevent entry. I walked along the row, glancing into them all. There was no food to be had from any of them, nor anything that could be conceivably used as a weapon. Though most of them were still furnished, removable commodities, such as sheets and blankets, had all been taken.

About two-thirds of the way along the line I encountered a bungalow that was empty of all furniture. Its doors were locked securely.

Intrigued, I broke in through a window and searched the house. In one of the back rooms I noticed that some of the floorboards had been removed and replaced. I levered them up with my knife.

In the space below there was a crate full of empty bottles. Someone had gouged a diagonal line across each of them with a file, thus weakening them. Close at hand was a folded pile of linen, torn into neat squares. In another room, also under the floorboards, I discovered ten five-gallon drums of petrol.

I considered the use of petrol bombs to us and whether it would be worth telling Rafiq about them. It was impossible for me to move them single-handed, and several men would have to come here to carry them away.

During the time I had been with Rafiq and the other refugees, there had been an endless rambling discussion about the kinds of weapons which would be of use to us. Rifles and guns were obviously the prime necessity, but they were impossible to find. It seemed unlikely we would ever obtain them except by accident, or somehow killing somebody else to take one. Then there would be the problem of ammunition. We all carried knives, though they were of assorted qualities. My own had formerly been a kitchen knife, which I had honed down to a usable size and sharpness.

The best use of a petrol bomb is to sling it as an anti-personnel device in an enclosed area. Narrow streets and houses were ideal. We were always in the countryside, in fields, lanes, woodlands. What use would we ever have for incendiaries?

I was searching for weapons and that's what the bottles were. I couldn't risk them falling into someone else's hands, or, perhaps worse, not telling Rafiq about them if later he found them. He would know I had missed them or hidden them. In the end I returned the bottles, linen and petrol to their hiding-places. If Rafiq disagreed with me about their possible usefulness, we could always come back here for them.

The lavatory was working and I used it. Afterwards I noticed that a bathroom cabinet on the wall still had its mirror intact and this gave me an idea. I prised it away and, using the glass-cutter, I sliced it up into long triangular strips. I managed to cut seven such strips from the thick glass. I fashioned the ends to as sharp a tine as possible, twice cutting myself in the process. I made rough handles for the daggers, using a chamois leather I had been carrying in my bag. I wrapped the leather in strips around the thicker ends.

I tried out one of the new daggers, swinging it experimentally in the air. It made a lethal but difficult weapon. They could be just as dangerous to whoever carried one of them, if he fell over, or if the glass broke while it was being swung. They needed a sheath of some kind.

I packed the seven new daggers into a heap, and prepared to roll them up into a piece of sacking so that I might carry them back to the others. As I did so, I noticed that one of the shards had a minute fault in the glass, near the handle.

I realized that it would shatter easily, lacerating the hand of whoever used it. I discarded it.

I was ready to return to Rafiq and the others. Night was falling, so I waited for the dark to come. The twilight was shorter than normal, because of the atmospheric murk and low clouds. When I felt it was safe to move, I collected my possessions and started back towards the encampment.

The time I had spent by the shore had had a strangely soothing effect on me. I wanted to spend more time there. I resolved to suggest it to Rafiq. Maybe we should set up some kind of encampment in the bungalows, or perhaps even join forces with those other refugees. I walked back, thinking how I might put this to Rafiq.

I was hiding at the top of a barn because my brother Clive had told me that the bogey was going to get me. I was about seven years old. Had I been a little older, of course I would probably have been able to control the irrational fear that took me. It was formless, but for the clear image of some monstrous being with black skin that was out to get me.

But at seven years old I cowered at the top of the barn, lying in my own private hidey-hole which no one knew was there. Where the farmer had stacked the bales of straw, a small cavity had been left between three of them and the roof.

The comforting subjective security of the hideout soon made me forget the bogey, and instead I lay in the warm straw thinking about something or other, a fantasy perhaps that involved aeroplanes and guns. When I heard rustling in the straw below my first panicky thoughts were of the bogey again, and I lay in a state of frozen terror while the rustling continued. Finally, I summoned courage to creep as silently as possible to the edge of my hideout and peer down.

In the loose straw on the ground at the back of the bales, a young man and a girl were lying with their arms around one another. The man was on top of the girl and the girl had her eyes closed. I did not know what they were doing.

After a few minutes, the young man moved slightly and made the girl remove her clothes. It seemed to me that she did not really want him to take them off, but she resisted only a little. They lay down again and she quickly helped him strip off his own clothes. I lay very still and quiet. When they were both naked he lay on top of her again and they began to make rasping noises with their throats. The girl's eyes were still closed, though her lids fluttered from time to time. I can't remember what I was thinking while I watched; I know I was curious to see a girl who could open her legs so wide. All the women I had ever known (my mother, my aunts, neighbours) had seemed incapable of opening their knees more than a few millimetres. I did not understand at all, but I was amazed at what they were doing and curious to know why. After a few more minutes the couple made a series of breathy screeching noises, then stopped moving around and lay together in silence. It was only then that the girl's eyes opened properly and looked up at me.

Many years later my brother Clive was among the first British National soldiers to be killed in action against the Afrims.

The words of the official at the UN camp came to mind as I drove along the North Circular Road. The radio confirmed that an amnesty had been offered by Tregarth's emergency cabinet, but the bulletin also said that the leaders of the Afrims were not responding positively. Another story described the interception of an arms ship in the Irish Sea, which the Navy had been forced to allow to pass as there were papers aboard showing the destination was Dun Laoghaire, in Ireland. The ship had later been seen close to the Pembrokeshire coast, where it was unloading several crates on to a number of launches.

The Afrims clearly had no reason to trust the British government's offer of an amnesty. Why should they? On several occasions in the past Tregarth or one of his ministers had introduced reforms that were intended to restrict the Afrims. There was no reason that now they had the upper hand militarily Tregarth's government would compromise with them. With the rift that already existed in the armed forces, and another threatened within the police forces, any policy of appeasement which was at all suspect would not work.

It was estimated that more than a quarter of the army had already seceded, and had placed itself at the disposal of the Afrim leaders in Yorkshire. Three ground-attack squadrons of the Royal Air Force had also changed allegiance.

In a later broadcast we heard a group of political pundits speculating that public sympathy for the Afrims was diminishing, and that Tregarth and his cabinet would take more militant action.

The only outward sign of the events taking place that we could discern was that traffic was unusually light. We were stopped several times by police patrols, but we had grown accustomed to this in the last few months and thought little of it. We were familiar with the appropriate responses to make to questions, and maintained a consistent story.

I was disturbed to notice that many of the police we encountered were from the civilian reserve special force. Stories describing various atrocities had been circulating, in particular one heard of black and coloured people being arrested without warrant and released only after a spell in police cells. Allegations of brutality were common. On the other hand, white people were subjected to harassment if known or suspected to be involved with anti-Afrim activities. The entire situation regarding the police was confused and inconsistent at this time, and I for one felt that it would not be an entirely bad thing if individual police forces were to divide formally so that everyone knew where they stood.

Just to the west of Finchley I had to stop the car and refill the tank with petrol. I was intending to use some of the petrol I had put by as a reserve, but discovered that during the night at the UN camp two of the cans had been emptied. I was forced to use up the whole of my reserve. I said nothing of this to Isobel or Sally, as I anticipated being able to restock sooner or later, even though none of the garages we had passed that day was open.

While I was pouring the petrol into the tank a man came out of a building close by, carrying a pistol and accused me of being an Afrim sympathizer. I asked him on what evidence he formed this suspicion, and he told me that no one could be driving a car at this time without the support of one political faction or another.

At the next police road block I reported this incident and was told to ignore it.

As we approached our house all three of us were revealing the apprehension we felt. Sally was restless and repeatedly asked to go to the toilet. Isobel smoked one cigarette after another and snapped irritably at me. I often found myself pushing up the speed of the car unconsciously, although I knew that it was better to stay at lower speeds.

To relieve the tension between us, I responded to Sally's requests by stopping the car at a public lavatory in the shopping area not far from where we lived, and while Isobel went inside with her I turned on the car radio and listened to another news bulletin.

Isobel said, when they had got back into the car, 'What shall we do if we can't get into the street?'

She had voiced the fear none of us had liked to express.

'I'm sure Nicholson will listen to reason,' I said.

'And if he doesn't?'

I didn't know.

I said, 'I just listened to the radio. They said that the Afrims were accepting the terms of the amnesty, but that occupation of empty houses was continuing.'

'What do they mean by empty?'

'I don't like to think.'

Behind us, Sally said, 'Daddy, are we nearly home?'

'Yes, dear,' Isobel said.

I started the engine and moved off. We reached the end of our street a few minutes later. The police and army trucks had gone but the barbed-wire barricade was still there. On the other side of the road, mounted on the top of a dark-blue van, was a television camera. One man stood by the camera, the other sat on the flat roof holding a large, flock-covered microphone on a boom. The camera was protected in front and at the sides by heavy plates of glass. Both men were wearing bulletproof vests.

I stopped the car a short distance from the barricade but left the engine running. No one appeared to be near the barricade. I blew the horn and regretted the action an instant later. Five men appeared from the house nearest to the barricade and walked towards us carrying rifles. They were Afrims.

'Oh God,' I said under my breath.

'Alan, go and talk to them. Perhaps our house is not being used by them!'

There was an edge of hysteria in her voice. Undecided, I sat in my seat and watched the men. They lined up at the barricade and stared at us without expression.

Isobel urged me again. I climbed out of the car and walked across to them.

I said, 'I live at number 47. Can we get through to our house, please?' They said nothing, but continued to stare. 'My daughter is ill. We must get her to bed.'

They stared.

I turned towards the TV crew and shouted, 'Can you tell me if anyone has been allowed in here today?'

Neither of them responded, although the man pointing the microphone in our direction looked down at his recording equipment and adjusted the setting of a knob.

I turned back to the Africans.

'Do you speak English?' I said. 'We must go to our house.'

There was a long silence, and then one of the men said in a thick accent, 'Go away!'

He lifted his rifle.

I hurried back to the car, put it into gear and accelerated away, swinging across the deserted road in a wide U-turn. As we passed the camera the Afrim fired his rifle and our windscreen shattered into opacity. I banged my forearm against it and a shower of glass fragments blew in. Isobel screamed and fell to the side, covering her head with her arms. Sally reached over from the back seat and put her arms around my neck and shouted incoherently into my ear.

When we came to the corner I slowed a little and leaned forward in my seat, pulling myself from Sally's grip. I looked in the rear-view mirror and saw that the TV crew had turned the camera to follow our flight down the road.

*

I stood with many others on the beach at Brighton. We were watching the old ship that was drifting in the Channel, listing to port at an angle of what the newspapers told us was twenty degrees. It was a long way offshore, riding the rough seas uneasily. The lifeboats from Hove, Brighton and Shoreham stood by, awaiting radio confirmation that they might take it in tow. Meanwhile, we on the shore were watching for it to sink, some of us having come a long distance to see the spectacle.

I reached the main group without meeting any patrols, and as soon as I considered it prudent I approached Rafiq and gave him the mirror daggers.

He said nothing about the other men who had been foraging, nor whether they had been successful.

He looked critically at the daggers but was unable to conceal his grudging admiration for my initiative. He took one in his right hand, balanced it, held it up, tried holstering it in his belt. His habitual frown deepened. I wanted to make excuses for the crudeness of the weapons, explain about the shortage of materials suitable for the manufacture of armaments, but held my silence as I knew he was aware of this.

His criticism of my handiwork was political, not practical.

Later, I saw him throwing away my daggers, and I decided against mentioning the petrol bombs.

As I passed through my adolescence I underwent like many boys of that age many puzzling stages of development towards full sexuality.

Near where I lived with my parents and brothers was a large area of waste ground which was cluttered with piles of building materials, and torn into mounds of bare earth by bulldozers. Local people said that the land had been sched-uled for housing development, but for reasons unknown to me the scheme had been delayed. While no building work went on the area provided an ideal playing ground for myself and my friends. Though officially we were forbidden to play there, the many hundreds of hiding-places made it possible for us to evade the various authority figures, such as parents, neighbours and the local police constable.

During this period I was undergoing doubts as to whether or not I should be indulging in such childish activities. My brother Clive had obtained a place at a good university and was halfway through his first year there. My younger brother Edward was at the same school as me, but he was bright and doing well with his lessons. I knew that if I wished to emulate Clive's achievement I should apply myself to my studies, but my mind and my body were occupied with an uncontrollable restlessness and many times I found myself on the building site with boys not only a year or two younger than I, but who attended a different school.

It had always appeared to me that the other boys were more advanced in their thinking than I was.

It was always they who made the suggestions about what we should do, and I who followed. Any move to some new hobby or activity came from someone else, and I was often amongst the last to take it up. In this way, anything I started to do was second-hand to me and I never really felt involved with it.

In a limbo between what I was and what I should be, I was doing neither well.

Accordingly, when two or three local girls joined us sometimes in the evenings, I was about the last to realize how their presence was affecting our behaviour, not only as a group but individually.

By chance, I knew one of these girls already. Her name was Tamsin. Her parents and mine were on friendly terms and we had passed several evenings in each other's company. However, whatever friendship might have formed between us was platonic and superficial: meeting a girl through your parents was the wrong way to do it. I had not reacted to her sexually at all. The first time she and her friends appeared on the building site I did not make anything of this small advantage I had over the other boys. On the contrary, I was embarrassed at her presence, imagining in some obscure way that word of my activities would get back to my parents. At first I pretended not to recognize her.

The first evening they were with us was awkward and unsettling. The conversation became an aimless and banal banter, with the girls feigning a lack of interest in us, while I and the other boys pretended to ignore them. This set the pattern for the next few encounters.

It happened that I went away with my parents for a short holiday and on my return I discovered that the relationship with the girls had entered a more physical phase. Some of the boys had air-rifles, and they were using these to try to impress the girls with their marksmanship. There was a lot of fake hostility and sometimes we would become involved in wrestling matches with them.

Even through this I failed to realize that it was a kind of preliminary sexual activity.

One evening a pack of cards was produced by one of the boys. For a while we played childish card games, but soon became bored. Then one of the girls said she knew a variety of the game Consequences which could be played with cards. She took the pack and dealt out cards to us all, explaining as she went. The idea was simple: everyone was dealt cards from the top of the pack, and the first boy and the first girl to receive a card of the same value – say two Queens or two Sevens – were matched up for Consequences.

I did not fully understand, but took the first card as it was given to me. It was a Three. On the first deal, no two people had similar cards, though one of the other boys also had a Three. This provoked rude comments, which I laughed at without properly appreciating the humour. On the next deal, Tamsin was dealt another Three.

A short discussion ensued, the outcome of which was that everyone decided I was the winner as I had drawn the Three before the other boy. I felt proud and terrified, a contradiction I could barely understand. I pretended I was willing to let him take my turn, as I did not realize what I was expected to do.

The girl who had started the game explained that it was usually played to the rules, and that I had to take my turn. I was to go, she said, to the far side of some nearby earthworks with Tamsin and we would be allowed ten minutes.

Tamsin and I stood up and amid many catcalls did as the girl had said. When we reached the other side of the earth works I felt I could not admit that I did not know what to do. Alone with a girl for the first time in my life I stood in miserable silence.

Then Tamsin said, 'Are you going to?'

I said, 'No.'

She sat down on the earth and I stood before her. I kept glancing at my watch.

I asked her several questions, the sort of things I should already have known if I hadn't always been so shy with her. I found out how old she was, for instance, and what her middle name was. She was a few months older than me. She told me the school she went to and what she was going to do when she left. In answer to my question, she told me that she had lots of boyfriends. When she asked me how many girlfriends I had I told her that there were a few.

As soon as the ten minutes were up we went back to the others.

I was handed the cards, which I shuffled and then dealt for the second round. This time there was no question as to who the winners were, as two Tens came up on the first deal. The boy and girl left us and went to the other side of the earthworks. While we waited for them to return, several dirty jokes were told. The atmosphere amongst those of us waiting was tense and strained, and although I joined in with the others I couldn't help wondering what was going on behind the mound of bare earth.

At the end of the ten minutes they had not returned. The girl who had started the game was the one with the boy and we assumed she would play by the rules. One of the boys suggested that we go and get them, and this we did, running towards the earthworks shouting and whistling. Before we reached them they came out and we went back to the cards. I noticed that neither of them looked at each other, nor at any of us.

On the third deal, Tamsin drew a number with one of the other boys and they went off to the mound. I suddenly hated this game! After a moment or two I declared I was sick of it and walked off in the direction of my house.

As soon as I was out of sight of the others, I worked round through the waste ground and approached the earthworks from the side. I was able to get close up to the couple without being observed, as a pile of unpainted window-frames was stacked nearby. From this cover I watched them.

They were standing up. Tamsin was wearing her school blazer and dress, as she had done all along. The boy was standing close to her, with his back to me. They were talking quietly.

Suddenly, he threw his arms around her neck and dragged her to the floor. They wrestled together for a moment, in the way we had often done before. At first she fought back, but after a minute or so she rolled away from him and lay passively. He reached over to her and laid his hand very tentatively on her stomach. Tamsin's head lolled away from him, facing towards my hiding-place, and I saw that her eyes were tightly closed. The boy pushed aside her blazer and I could see the gentle swell of her breasts by his hand. Because she was lying down, they were not as protuberant as normal. The boy was staring at them rigidly and I discovered that I was beginning to have an erection. With my hand in my trouser pocket I moved my penis so that it was less uncomfortable, and as I did so the boy's hand slid up and cupped one of her breasts. He slid the hand backwards and forwards with increasing speed. In a while, Tamsin cried out as if it were hurting her, and she rolled back towards him. Though she then had her back to me, I could see that she had put her hand at the top of his legs and was caressing him.

I was becoming excited by this, and though I wanted to stay where I was I felt very unsettled by what I was witnessing. I backed away and walked in the direction I had come. As I did so my hand was still in my pocket holding my penis, and in a moment I ejaculated. I mopped myself clean with a handkerchief, then went back to the others, explaining that I had returned home but that my parents were out.

A few minutes later Tamsin and the boy came back to the group. Like the others, they avoided looking at us.

We were prepared for a fourth hand, but the girls said they were fed up and wanted to go home. We tried to persuade them to stay but in a few moments they left. As they walked

41

away we could hear them giggling. When he was sure they were gone, the boy who had just come back undid the fly of his trousers and showed us his penis. It was still erect and looked a dark red colour. He masturbated in front of us and we watched enviously.

The girls came back to the building site the following evening, by which time I had devised a method of ensuring I dealt myself the right cards. I rubbed the breasts of each of the three girls, and one of them allowed me to put my hand inside her dress and bra and feel her nipples. After this the cards were no longer used and we took it in turns. By the end of the following week I had had sexual intercourse with Tamsin, and was proud that I was the only one of us she would do it with.

I took my examinations in the weeks following and was not successful. I had to buckle down to work properly and re-take the papers. In the course of time I lost contact with the group. I entered university two years later. Before I moved away from home, I saw Tamsin twice more. Both times were within the families, but she would not meet my eyes.

If anything, the wind had increased in the time I had been on the beach, and as the waves broke on the shingle close to where we were standing, a fine spray was driven across our faces. I was wearing my spectacles. Within a few minutes the lenses were misted with a thin deposit of salt. I removed them and placed them inside my pocket in their case.

The sea was now rough, white breakers flickering across its surface as far as the horizon. As yet the sun still shone, though there was a bank of dark cloud in the south-west. I stood in a large crowd of people, and we were watching the drifting ship.

The transistor radio carried by someone announced the

news that the ship was not to be assisted by rescue craft, and that the lifeboats were being ordered to return to their stations. Those of us on the beach could see those actual boats circling, the crews obviously undecided whether to obey the orders from the shore or to follow their deep-rooted sense of duty to stricken ships. Some distance behind the drifting ship we could see the Royal Navy frigate which had arrived while we were watching from the shore. So far it had not interfered, but it was moving steadily closer.

I knew the beach behind me was crowded. I turned round to try to estimate the number of people who had come to watch, but it was now a huge crowd and I was too low down to see well. Every available access point along the side of the King's Road and the raised promenade was packed. In addition, hundreds more people stood on Palace Pier, hanging over the rails, watching the damaged ship.

At just after four minutes past two o'clock the lifeboats turned away from the ship and headed back to their respective stations. I estimated that in less than a quarter of an hour the ship would have drifted past the end of the pier and be invisible from where I was standing. I debated whether or not to move, but decided to stay.

The ship sank at just before ten past. Its angle of list had increased markedly in the last few minutes. Many of the people on board could be seen jumping over the side. The ship sank quickly and unspectacularly. I was horrified by the noise it made: a huge, hollow, deep-rooted belching of air from within.

Once the ship had disappeared, and all trace of it on the surface of the sea was overtaken by the rough swell, many of the onlookers began to disperse. Within fifteen minutes most of the crowd had gone. I stayed on, enthralled in some way I could not quite understand by the feel of the wind,

43

the sound and the sight of the waves and by the memory of what I had witnessed. I had never before seen a ship go down.

I left the beach an hour or so later, distressed by the appearance of the few Africans who were managing to struggle to the shore. Ambulance staff and other humanitarian workers were waiting to take care of them, but no one went out into the breakers to try to help. Fewer than fifty of the boat people made it to the beach alive. I understand from my acquaintances in Brighton that in the next few days the sea threw up hundreds of dead with every tide. Human flotsam, made buoyant by its distended, gas-filled belly.

As night fell I pulled the car into the side of the road and brought it to a halt. It was too cold to continue driving with the glass of the broken windscreen knocked away, and in any case I was again running low on petrol. I did not want to discuss this with Isobel in front of Sally.

For security we had driven north from London and were in the countryside around Cuffley. I had debated internally about whether to try to reach the UN camp again, but after two long and extremely tiring journeys in the last twenty-four hours, we were not anxious to go back there if there was any alternative at all. Anyway, the dwindling supply of petrol and the memory of the discouraging official that morning both suggested we should at least try to find an alternative.

We took our warmest clothes from the suitcases and put them on. Sally lay down on the back seat of the car and we covered her with as much warm material as we could find. Isobel and I waited in silence, smoking the last of our cigarettes, until we felt reasonably sure she had drifted off into sleep. None of us had eaten a proper meal during the day, the only food we had consumed being some chocolate we found in an automatic machine outside a row of closed shops. While we sat there it began to rain, and in a few minutes a trickle of water came in through the empty rubber frame, and ran over the dashboard on to the floor.

'We'd better make for Bristol,' I said.

'What about our house?'

I shook my head. 'There's no hope of going back.'

'I don't think we should go to Bristol.'

'Where else can we go?'

'Back to the UN camp. At least, for the next few days.'

'And after that?'

'I don't know. Things *must* get better. We can't be kicked out of our house just like that. There must be a law ...'

I said, 'That won't be the answer. Things have gone too far now. The Afrim situation has made the housing shortage much worse. I can't see them agreeing to a deal in which they would have to give up houses they've already taken over.'

Isobel said, 'All right.'

I didn't say any more. In the last few weeks Isobel had shown an increasing denial about the developing problem of the African refugees, and this had only widened the distance between us. Whereas whenever I left the house or went to my job I was continually faced with the disintegration of the society that we knew, Isobel appeared to withdraw from the reality as if she could survive what was going on simply by ignoring it. Even now, with our home lost to us, she was content to allow me to take the decisions.

Before we settled for the night, I walked from the car in the direction of a nearby house, from whose windows showed warm amber light. As I walked through the gates an unaccountable fear came into my mind and I turned away.

The house had a solid, respectable look, an intruder flood-light came on as soon as I approached. I remembered how I must look to others: unshaven and in need of a change of clothing. It was difficult to say what reception I would have received from the occupiers of the house had I knocked at the door. The anarchy of the situation in London bore no relation to this area, which had as yet had no contact with the homeless and militant African people.

I returned to the car.

'We're going to a hotel for the night,' I said.

Isobel made no answer, but stared out of her side window into the dark.

'Well, don't you care?'

'No.'

'What do you want to do?'

'We'll be all right here.'

The rain still dribbled into the car through the gaping hole that had been our windscreen. In the few minutes I had been outside, the drizzle had soaked my outer clothes. I wanted Isobel to touch me, share to some measure the experience of my walk ... yet I shrank mentally from the thought of her hand touching my arm.

'What about Sally?' I said.

'She's asleep. If you want to find a hotel, I won't object. Can we afford it?'

'Yes.'

I thought about it for a bit longer. We could stay here, or we could drive on. I glanced at my watch. It was just after eight o'clock. If we slept in the car, in what kind of condition would we be by morning?

I started the engine and drove slowly back to the centre of Cuffley. I did not know any hotels in the neighbourhood, but was confident we would find somewhere. The first place

46

we found was full, and so was the second. We were following directions to a third when the petrol-tank finally ran dry. I coasted the car into the side and stopped.

I was relieved in a way that the decision had been made for us. I'd held out no real hopes of finding a hotel that would offer us a room – at both of the two places I had tried I felt I was being sized up. Maybe both those hotels had empty rooms that they were not willing to let us use. Isobel said nothing, but sat with her eyes closed. Her face and clothes were damp from the rain which had blown in through the screen.

I ran the heater until the water inside the mechanism had cooled to a point where there was no more benefit to be had. Isobel said she was tired.

We agreed to take it in turns to lie across one another. I said she could do it first. She tucked her knees up and lay across from her seat with her head in my lap. I put my arms around her to keep her warm, then tried to find a comfortable position myself.

Within a few minutes Isobel had passed into a semblance of sleep. I spent the night uneasily, feeling cold, uncomfortable, damp. My neck and back ached, while Isobel and Sally slept or seemed to. Behind us the child stirred from time to time. Of the three of us she was probably the only one who rested fully in the night.

Rafiq showed me a leaflet he had found. It was printed by the Royal Secessionist Air Force, and it stated that ten minutes' warning, in the form of three low traverses, would always be given to civilian occupants of villages before a raid took place.

*

There was a road through the New Forest. I drove along it in the twilight of the evening, knowing that we had stayed away too long. It had not anyway been wise to do what we had done, and with the present police situation it had been foolhardy.

I had a girl in the car with me. Her name was Patti. She and I had been at a hotel in Lymington and we were hurrying to get back to London before nine o'clock. She was asleep next to me, her head resting lightly on my shoulder.

She was awakened by my stopping the car at a road block on the outskirts of Southampton. There were several men standing by the barricade, which was a makeshift arrangement of two old cars and an assortment of heavy building materials. Each of the men carried a weapon, though only one had a rifle. It occurred to me that for the last half-hour we had not seen any traffic going in the same direction as us. I realized then most local people would probably have known about the blockade, and have found an alternative route.

As a result of the road block we had to turn around and follow a long diversion through the countryside to Winchester, and thence to the main road to London. We had been warned by the people at the hotel to expect similar obstructions at Basingstoke and Camberley and as it turned out we were required to make lengthy detours around these also.

The road into south-west London was unobstructed by civilian defence groups, but we saw many police vehicles and spot checks on motorists. We were fortunate in passing through without delay. I had not been outside London for several months and had no idea that access and movement had been curtailed to this degree.

I dropped Patti near the flat she shared in Barons Court

and carried on towards my home in Southgate. Again, none of the major roads was blocked by civilian resistance groups, but I was stopped by the police near King's Cross and my possessions were searched.

It wasn't until nearly one in the morning that I arrived home. Isobel had not waited up for me.

The next morning I went to a nearby house and managed to persuade the occupier to let me have some petrol siphoned from his car's tank. I paid him well for it. He told me there was a garage a short distance down the road which had been selling petrol up until the night before. He gave me directions on how to find it.

I returned to the car and told Isobel and Sally that with any luck we would be able to make Bristol during the day.

Isobel said nothing, although I knew she did not want to go to her parents. From my point of view it was the only solution. As it was equally obvious that we could no longer return to our house, the prospect of driving to Bristol, distant from London but familiar to both of us from many family visits, was a reassuring one.

I poured the petrol into the tank and started the engine. As we drove towards the garage I had been told about, we listened to a news broadcast on the radio. This revealed that several divisions of West Mercia Police had seceded to the Afrim side, the first publicly acknowledged split. About a quarter of the force had broken away. There was to be a meeting of chief constables with both the Afrim command and the Home Office, and a statement would be issued from Whitehall later in the day.

We found the garage and were allowed what the proprietor informed us was the standard quota: five pounds' worth. With what we had, this gave us just sufficient petrol in the car for us to reach Bristol, provided we were not forced to make too many detours.

I told Isobel and Sally, to their great relief. We agreed to set off as soon as we had found something to eat.

At Potters Bar we went to a small café which gave us a good breakfast at normal prices. No mention was made of the Afrim situation, and the radio that was playing carried only light music. At Isobel's request we were sold a vacuum-flask which they filled for us with hot coffee, and after we had washed in the toilets of the café we set out.

The day was not warm but there was no rain. Driving with the windscreen missing was unpleasant but not impossible. I decided not to listen to the radio, seeing for once some wisdom in Isobel's attitude of not allowing the events around us to affect us. Although it was of course essential to keep abreast of the developing situation, I was won over to her passivity.

A new worry materialized in the form of a continual vibration from the engine. I had been unable to maintain regular servicing on it, and I knew that one of the valves was in need of replacement. I trusted to it lasting at least until we reached Bristol and did not mention it to the others.

As far as I could see, the worst part of the journey would be in avoiding barricaded sections of the suburbs around London. I therefore skirted the north-western edge of the city, driving first to Watford (unbarricaded), then to Rickmansworth (barricaded, but open to through traffic on the by-pass), and then across country to Amersham, High Wycombe and south towards Henley-on-Thames. As we went further from London we saw fewer and fewer overt signs of the trouble and a mood of tranquillity came over us. We were even able to purchase more petrol and fill our reserve cans.

At another small café on the way into Reading we ate a lunch and made our way towards the main road to Bristol, confident of arriving there well before nightfall.

We were driving away from Reading in a westerly direction when the engine vibrations increased suddenly and the power faded. I kept the car going as long as possible but at the first incline it stopped. I did what I could to investigate but the fuel and ignition systems were not faulty. I knew that the valve had finally blown.

I was on the point of discussing this with Isobel and Sally when a police car pulled up alongside.

I worked for some months as part-time barman in a public house in the East End of London. It had become necessary to earn some extra money. I was then studying for my Finals and my grant had already been spent.

It came as something of a surprise for me to learn that the East End was a series of loosely connected communities, a mix of almost every conceivable race and creed. Until I started the job I had always assumed that this part of London was primarily English, or white. The pub reflected this cosmopolitan aspect to a certain extent, although it was clear that the publican did not encourage it. Arguments in the bar often arose. We had been instructed to remove bottles and glasses from the counters if a fracas developed. It was part of my duties as barman to assist in breaking up any fight that started.

When I had been at the pub for three months the publican decided to hire a pop group for the weekends, and in no time at all the trouble had passed. The type of customer changed noticeably.

Instead of the older drinker, set in his ways and dogmatically opinionated, the pub began to attract a younger element. Members of the minority groups stayed away and within a couple of months almost every customer at the pub was aged less than thirty.

The clothing fashions at the time tended to be colourful and casual, but those sort of clothes were rarely seen at the pub. Most of the men wore suits or jackets, without neckties, and the young women wore conventional dresses. I soon learned that this was an outward manifestation of an innate conservatism that was widespread in that part of London.

The publican's first name was Harry; I never learned his surname. He had once been a professional wrestler and on the wall of the bar behind the counter there were several photographs of him in satin dressing-gowns and with a long pigtail. I never heard Harry talk about his experiences in the ring, though his wife once mentioned that he had earned enough money from it to enable him to buy the pub outright.

Sometimes at weekends, several of Harry's friends would come to the bar for after-hours drinking. Most of these people were about his own age. On these occasions he would offer me a few extra shillings to stay late and serve them. As a result of this I overheard many of their conversations and came to learn that their prejudices and information on subjects such as race and politics were as conservative as those attitudes implied by the dress of the other customers.

Several years later, John Tregarth and his party were to gain a substantial electoral backing from areas in which different races were mixed.

We stayed a few more days at the encampment after the women were abducted. None of us could decide what should be done. Most of us had lost a wife or a partner in the raid. We knew that it would be no good to approach the Afrims directly. We all felt the same instinct, which was to stay close to the place from where they had been taken. I felt impatient and ineffectual, and worried continually about what might be happening to Sally. I was less concerned for Isobel, I confess. It was not a time for rational thinking – it took all my effort to get though each day, struggling with a sense of loss, guilt, concern, utter despair. It was with something close to relief, then, that I heard a rumour that we were about to break camp. One of the men said he had heard Rafiq say it was time for another visit to Augustin's.

Although I felt no urgency myself to visit the place, it did at least mean that the period of inaction was at an end. We were going to be busy, packing up the handcarts, moving on. As we started these preparations Rafiq came across to me and confirmed the rumour about Augustin's. It would, he said, be good for the morale of the men.

He appeared to be right, as within a couple of hours the mood had changed, and in spite of a sharp fall in temperature we walked for the first hour in a spirit of cavalier good humour.

'You do have a name?' I said.
   'Yes.'
   'Are you going to tell me what it is?'
   'No.'
   'Go on ... what is it?'
   'I don't want to say. What's your name?'
   'Alan. Come on.'
   'I don't want to.'
   'Do you have a good reason for withholding this information?'
   'Yes. That is, no.'
   'Well, tell me then.'

'No.'

That is the first conversation I had with my wife, setting a sort of marker. Her name was Isobel. We were both nineteen then.

The news of what was happening in Africa did not come as a surprise – the disputes over land, food, water and mineral resources had been worsening for years. But no one could have anticipated the scale of the disaster, and feelings of profound shock reverberated around the world. The consequences were on a global scale.

It soon became clear that nowhere in the world would escape the fall-out from Africa. In Britain, a mood settled on the country as people realized that their lives were going to change for ever when, inevitably, some of the refugees would reach us. It made me think of my parents' descriptions of what had happened in Britain in the early months of the Second World War. On the surface everything appeared to go on as normal: shops stayed open, international flights came and went, trains and buses continued to run, you could still fill your car with petrol, carry on with your job, go on holiday abroad. But private conversations were dominated by one subject: the appalling casualties and destruction in the African countries caused by the war that raged across the continent, followed by the inevitable humanitarian and refugee crisis. Then, latterly, as we should have predicted but no one quite did, the impact of hundreds of thousands of those refugees flooding into the country.

It was the students at the college who first brought home to me the immediacy of what was happening. We had many foreign exchange students and a large proportion of these came from African nations. Naturally, they were concerned on a personal level, but the wider cause was taken up by all the students. Nor was it just at my college. Universities across the country were brought to a standstill by the students' persistent demands that the authorities take effective action to give aid to the refugees.

Coping with the student demands soon became my daily preoccupation. Meanwhile, at home, it was as if nothing was happening in the outside world. Isobel was determined to bury her head in the sand. She seemed to be paralysed by shock, and would not talk about the international situation at all.

As the refugee crisis deepened newspapers, radio and television poured out a stream of official advice, warnings, and the introduction of emergency powers. Immense social, economic and political emergencies broke around us. There were frequent appeals for calm behaviour, volunteers to come forward to assist with humanitarian work, and announcements about imminent restrictions on travel abroad and the purchase of foreign currency or assets, the possibility of conscription, even the introduction of quotas and rationing. Food itself was not rationed, but the available choice in shops became increasingly restricted. Much shorter opening hours were allowed in pubs and restaurants. Communities were encouraged to set up self-administering guard patrols. The police were allowed to carry firearms. Taxes went up: at first the increases were gradual, but within a few months most people were paying twice as much tax as before.

Through this we carried on as normally as possible, as everyone around us was doing. Day-to-day concerns continued. On one level my own life was no different from before: during the worst of the African war crisis I was involved in a passionate affair with a third-year student called Lucilla. With hindsight it seems unbelievable that such an affair could happen at a time of national emergency, but at the time everyone was intent on acting as if life would continue as it always had. For me, Lucilla symbolized that wish. She tired of me suddenly, though, dropping me in a traumatic way just at the point where Isobel was trying to convince me we should sell our house and move out of London. I handled all that badly.

After the third refugee ship arrived in British waters the intense pressure on housing was an immediate concern, resolving our personal decision about whether or not to move house. Buying or selling houses in the large cities was abruptly prohibited under the emergency powers, except under official supervision.

The coastline soon became the focus of everyone's interest. We had all heard of the big ships arriving, but around the British coastline small boats were landing day and night. Many of the refugees who were rounded up were put in old government-owned buildings: disused army bases, airfields, military hospitals, training camps, even a former prison, but the majority of the people were not found, or somehow eluded the immigration officers, and so were not given official help. These refugees tended to gravitate to the big cities, where local authorities struggled to find them accommodation.

Inevitably, there was a minority of the population who reacted with hatred and aggression to these desperate and dispossessed people. There were many reports of assaults in the street, gangs of youths prowling the cities at night, and arson attacks on buildings where the immigrants were known to be housed. However, the majority of British people had nothing to do with this. The traditional values of tolerance continued, but it was impossible not to be aware of what was happening in every part of the country.

Almost everyone I knew or spoke to during this period

expressed the same concerns. They were appalled at what had happened to the refugees, the circumstances in which they had escaped from their own countries and the conditions in which they were now living. Ordinary people did what they could to assist the volunteer and government agencies rehouse or resettle the people, but at the same time they could not help but fear for the impact nearly two million homeless refugees might have on their own lives, homes and jobs. They could hardly imagine the changes that would follow at the schools their children went to, the hospitals they needed to use, and so on. Most of those ordinary British people, tolerant in outlook, dealt with their fears by looking away, hoping the problem would sort itself out. I began to understand Isobel's reaction better.

So I gradually became one of those people too, and at my college and in my department I was surrounded by others like me.

In line with many other tertiary establishments throughout the country, our college formed a fundraising society to try to help the plight of the Africans. Our motives were principally humanitarian but we made membership open to all. Because we did so, we found there were others with a less liberal outlook, who moved into our meetings and used our network of contacts to spread their own views. The addresses we had obtained of welfare groups, for example, were passed to extreme right-wing organizations known for their opposition to the amnesty for illegal entrants. Disillusioned and disappointed, our short-lived society dispersed. I realized that we were blinding ourselves to the change that was taking place in people's attitudes.

There were now so many stories of violent attacks on both sides that they could no longer be pretended away as a minor issue. Most of these incidents seemed acceptably far away, in other cities, but when two young men were stabbed to death a short walk from our house I knew it was no longer possible to ignore what was going on. During a weekend trip to Bristol, to visit Isobel's parents, our journeys to and fro were interrupted several times by police checks and army road blocks. The countryside, for so long a symbol of peace and harmony in Britain, now felt as if it was a landscape laced with traps and menace.

Rumours began, and they helped explain certain incidents the authorities had tried to deny had happened. One of these stories was that some of the African immigrants were forming themselves into armed militias, that they appeared to be receiving shipments of weapons from abroad and that they were moving into cities and occupying houses and displacing the former inhabitants.

In the remaining days of the semester my colleagues and I did what we could to exchange our beliefs with our students. They too had much to tell us. Then the end of term arrived.

Industrial unrest spread and public demonstrations in the streets became an everyday event. During those weeks after the closure of the college I saw that we had been wrong. Attempting to arouse sympathy for the Afrims was not going to work. There was a small and vociferous section of the community which stuck to liberal principles, but more and more ordinary people were coming into direct conflict with the Afrims as the armed insurgence went on.

At one of the largest demonstrations in London I saw some of the students from the college carrying a large banner emblazoned with the name of our society. I had not intended to join the march, but I left the side of the road and followed the demonstration to its noisy and violent conclusion.

In the event, the doors of the college never reopened for the following semester.

The two police officers told us we were in restricted territory and that we must move on at once. There were reports, they said, that there had been a mutiny in an army camp and that the entire neighbourhood was being sealed off by government forces.

I told the police that our car had broken down and that though we were not disputing what they told us, we had come into the vicinity without any warning from the authorities.

The policemen appeared to be incapable of listening to reason.

They repeated their instructions and told us again to leave the area immediately. Sally began to cry at this point as one of the policemen had opened the door of the car and dragged her out. I protested at once and was hit hard across my face with the back of a hand.

They pressed me up against the side of the car and searched my pockets. When they looked in my wallet and saw that I had once been a lecturer at the college they confiscated my identity card. I protested, but they ignored me.

Isobel and Sally were also searched.

When this was completed the police took our belongings from the car and put them in the road. They took our reserve petrol cans from the boot and placed them inside the police car. I remembered what I had heard on the radio earlier, and asked to see the warrant cards of the police. Again they ignored me.

One of them gave me a slip of paper. One side had a pre-printed receipt, acknowledging that they had seized materials and artefacts from me, which although considered illegal would be returned after completion of the procedure described on the other side.

The other side was simply printed with a telephone number, and the words, *Police Investigation Unit.*

They told us they would be returning along this road in half an hour. We were to be gone by then. Otherwise, they said, they would not be responsible for anything that might happen.

As they turned to get back into their car, I moved forward quickly and kicked the man who had hit me. I got my shoe hard against the base of his spine, throwing him forward on to the ground. I had never in my life done anything like that before. I was thrilled by the sensation of fear and excitement that suddenly coursed through me. The other cop turned round and dived at me. I swung my fist at his face, but missed. In that frozen split second I saw that he had not shaved for at least three days. He threw an arm around my neck, pulled me to the ground and held me there with my arm twisted up against my back and my face pressed painfully into the dirt. The man I had attacked climbed to his feet. He came over and placed three hard kicks into my side.

With the third one I managed to get hold of the cop's leg with my free arm, and held it for a couple of seconds before he pulled it away. I realized then that he was wearing soft white running shoes.

The other policeman had no insignia or identifying number on his jacket. He released me, and I collapsed face-down on the road.

When they had gone Isobel helped me on to the front passenger seat of the car. She wiped away some of the blood that was coming out of my mouth, using a paper tissue.

As soon as I had recovered sufficiently to walk we set off across a field in a direction opposite to the one in which the police had waved vaguely when telling us about the army mutiny.

There was a severe pain in my side and although I could walk with some difficulty I was unable to carry anything heavy. Breathing was difficult, I was fearful that the man who kicked me might have broken some ribs. However, I knew that the injuries would have been much worse if he had been wearing boots or even leather shoes.

Isobel therefore had to take our two large suitcases, while Sally carried the small one. I held our portable radio under my arm. As we walked I switched it on, but was able to raise only one BBC channel and that was the one playing light music.

All three of us were at the point of despair. Neither Isobel nor Sally asked me what we should do next. For the first time since leaving our house we were wholly aware how far beyond our control events were moving. Later, the rain returned and we sat under a tree on the edge of a field, frightened, directionless, and utterly involved in a sequence of events that no one had expected and that no one now was able to stop.

I learned from reading the *Guardian* that the country was polarizing into three general groups. As newspapers tend to influence the outlook of their readership over a long period of time, the article summed up changes that I had been aware of myself.

Firstly, there were those people who had already come into direct contact with the Afrims and had a personal grievance, or those people who were racially prejudiced in any case. These people supported the government policy of rounding up African refugees whenever possible, and deporting them en masse.

Secondly, there were those people who maintained that Britain's social heritage was based on integration and tolerance, that as a wealthy industrialized country Britain was able to bear the financial costs of giving shelter to these people, and that in the long term the upheaval caused by the arrival of so many would pass and absorption into British life would produce a benefit. This was the opinion held by the leader writers at the *Guardian*, and although the newspaper reported events and news stories objectively it was an editorial outlook that was maintained throughout the long early period of the crisis.

Thirdly, there were those people who did not care whether or not the Africans landed, armed themselves, formed themselves into bands of militia, took over other people's homes, so long as they themselves were not directly affected by anything these new arrivals did.

I knew that my general lack of involvement, encouraged by Isobel's continual denial of what was going on around us, placed me as a member of this third group.

I questioned my own moral stand. Although my instinct was to remain uncommitted and uninvolved – at this time I was involved in an absorbing affair with a young woman called Eloise, and she was distractingly taking up most of my time and thoughts – it was this awareness of my own insularity which troubled me. In the end it convinced me I should join the pro-Afrim society at the college.

Political and social climates in the country were not responsive to the kind of moral judgements that had to be made.

Soon after the second election, Tregarth's government introduced much of the new legislation it had promised in its manifesto. The police were given wider powers of search, entry and detention, and the elements that Tregarth's ministers described as subversive were more effectively dealt with. Public demonstrations on any political issue were tightly controlled by the police, and the armed forces were assigned to assist in the keeping of the peace.

As the boats from Africa continued to land on British shores, the problem could no longer be ignored.

After the first wave of landings the government issued the warning that illegal immigrants would be prevented from landing, forcibly if necessary. This led directly to the Poole incident in Dorset, where the army confronted two ship-loads of African refugees. News of the approaching ships had leaked out into the media, and thousands of people travelled from all over the country to Poole, to witness the landing. The result was a violent confrontation between army and public. The Afrims came ashore.

After this, the government's warning was modified to the effect that as illegal immigrants were captured they would be given suitable treatment in hospital, then deported.

In the meantime, polarization of attitudes was accelerated by the illegal supply of arms to the Afrims. The official version was that foreign powers were illegally supplying weapons, in an attempt to destabilize the country. The reality was that there were many factions within the country prepared to help the refugees. But with the coming of the armed militias the schisms in the country grew ever deeper.

The private life of everyone in the regions directly affected – and of many in areas away from the insurgence – revolved entirely around the immediate problem. The police force divided, and so did the Army and Air Force. The Navy remained loyal to the government. When a detachment of American Marines was landed to act in an advisory capacity to what had become known as the Nationalist side, and when the United Nations drafted a peacekeeping force, the military aspect of the situation became resolved.

By this time, no one could be said to be uninvolved.

'I hear we're going to Augustin's.'

The man marching next to me stared straight ahead. 'About bloody time.'

'You been missing it then?'

'Piss off, will you?'

I said nothing, but let them drag out the interplay of ideas to their logical conclusion. I'd heard this or a similar conversation a dozen times in the last week.

'It was Rafiq that decided. The others wanted to stay put.'

'I know. Good old Raf.'

'He's missing it, too.'

'They got one of his? He never mentions it.'

'Yeah. They say he was screwing Olderton's wife on the quiet.'

'I don't believe it.'

'It's a fact.'

'What about Olderton, then?'

'Never knew a thing.'

The other man laughed. 'You're right. I have been missing it.'

'Haven't we all.'

They both laughed then, cackling like two old women in the uncanny cold silence of the countryside.

We slept fitfully that night in the open air. Fortunately there was no rain, and although we were all cold and uncomfortable, nothing went seriously wrong. In the morning we were lucky to find a shop that sold us, at normal prices, most of the camping equipment we needed. At this stage we still had not come up with a plan, beyond the fact that we all agreed that we must get to Bristol as soon as we could.

We walked all that day, finally pitching camp under some trees that grew alongside a farmer's field. It rained during the night, but this time we were adequately protected. Things suddenly did not feel so black as they had done a day or so before. In spite of what at first seemed to be great difficulties, our spirits stayed high. That night, when I overheard Isobel talking with Sally shortly before the girl fell asleep, I detected a strain of false optimism in their tone. It was almost as if they were speaking for my benefit.

As far as I was concerned, I was passing through what I was to learn later was a temporary phase of genuine high spirits. Paradoxical as this may seem, the comparative freedom we now enjoyed, at a time when the martial law in the cities was imposing impossible restrictions on most people, compensated for a lot. Or so it felt. We had lost virtually all our personal possessions, were now homeless and the possibility of reaching Bristol was as remote as ever. None of us mentioned any of this again.

The next night we came across a stretch of woodland, a mixture of tall trees and areas of tangled undergrowth that would provide shelter as well helping to conceal us. We made our encampment there for a few days. It was during this time that our mood became depressed.

For food and other essentials we went to a village half an hour's walk away across the fields. Here we could buy everything we needed without anyone asking questions. Later in the week, though, a detachment of the Afrim forces raided the village. After that the people who lived in the village put up barricades, and this source of supply was cut off from us.

We decided we had to move on. We travelled across the

countryside in a southerly direction. I became increasingly aware of Isobel's unspoken resentment about what was happening to us, and I found myself competing with her for Sally's approval. In this way, Sally became the instrument of our conflict, as in fact she had always been, and suffered as a result.

The day after the soaking of our equipment and possessions in the crossing of the river, the conflict between us came to a head.

By this time we felt as if we were entirely out of touch with the rest of the world. The batteries of the radio had been growing steadily weaker, and now the water had damaged it beyond our repair. While Isobel and Sally laid out our clothes and equipment to dry in the sun, I went off by myself and tried to concentrate my thoughts into something from which I could plan our next moves.

Cut off from news, we knew only what our own situation was. It was more or less hopeless, but none of us said that aloud. I felt we would have been better placed to cope with our own troubles if we had been able to keep up with the current state of political developments. We often saw military trucks driven down the roads at high speeds, and there were many helicopters, night and day. We always took cover, if we could, when a copter went over.

Much later I learned that during this period there was a large-scale humanitarian exercise being put into effect by the Red Cross and the United Nations. This was attempting to trace and rehabilitate all those people like ourselves who had been dispossessed by the fighting. I don't know how many people they were able to help – we never saw anything of that sort going on. As events turned out, this relief effort was destined to fail. With the worsening state of the conflict, and the increasing social chaos caused by so many houses being forcibly taken over, and the damage to many more by the shelling, both welfare organizations became discredited in the mind of the public. This was partly because their work was cynically used by all combatants as a tactical, political or social weapon against the others. There were also several incidents in which Red Cross workers came under fire, and they took many casualties. A massive distrust arose of all humanitarian or relief organizations and in time they scaled down their activities, soon becoming more of a token presence than any practical help to the victims of the war.

It was difficult to reconcile ourselves to the standard of existence we were now having to accept.

I found myself looking at the situation as being in a sense predetermined. It seemed to me that my attitude to Isobel, and the way in which our marriage had become nothing more than a social convenience, had been forced into resolution by what was happening to us. While we had been together at our house, living a normal suburban life, on a day-to-day basis we had been able to disregard what had happened to us. Our marriage had become a sham, a convenience to us both, even if we never admitted it. But now we had been forced into this state of bare subsistence, constantly feeling in danger, undecided what to do next, we could no longer pretend about ourselves.

In those few minutes alone I saw with penetrating clarity that our marriage had reached its conclusion and that the moment had arrived when the pretence must be abandoned. Practical considerations tried to intrude but I ignored them. Isobel could fend for herself, or surrender herself to the police. Sally could come with me. We would return to London, and from there decide what next to do.

For one of the few times in my life I had reached a positive decision by myself, and it was a harsh one I did not like.

Memories of some of what Isobel and I had meant to each other – many of them good memories – pulled at me. But I still had the bruises from the policeman's kicking in my side. They alone were a constant reminder of what our lives had become.

The past had moved away from us and so had the present. Those moments with Isobel when I had thought we might once again work out a way to live with each other seemed now to be falsehoods. Regret did not exist.

We were due to arrive at Augustin's the following day, but for various reasons we had to spend one more night in a field. None of us liked sleeping in the open, preferring to find abandoned houses or farm buildings. I never found it easy to settle when on hard ground and exposed to the cold. In addition, that night we discovered around midnight, too late to move away, that by chance we had camped not far from an anti-aircraft emplacement. Several times the guns opened fire and rockets were launched, and although searchlights were used twice we were unable to see at what it was they were firing.

We moved on at first light, every one of us cold, irritable and tired. While we were still a couple of hours away from Augustin's we were stopped by a patrol of US Marines, and searched. It was routine, perfunctory, and it was over in ten minutes.

Sobered from garrulous irritability to our habitual watchful silence, we arrived in the vicinity of Augustin's around midday.

Rafiq detailed myself and two others to move on ahead and establish that the camp was still there. All we had by way of directions was an Ordnance Survey grid reference which had been passed on to us along the traveller network.

Although we had no reason to doubt the information – the network was the only reliable form of news dissemination – there was always the chance that one or another of the military groups had moved it on. In any case, it was customary to make sure that at the time we were there we would not interrupt anyone or be interrupted.

While Rafiq organized the setting up of a camp, and preparation of a meal, we moved forward.

The grid reference turned out to be a field which once had been used for crops. It had apparently lain fallow for some time, at least for more than a year, as it was overgrown with rank grass and weeds. There were still traces of old stubble underfoot. Although there were several signs of human habitation – a soil latrine in one corner, many bare patches in the grass, a refuse tip, the burnt ulcers where open fires had been – the field was now unoccupied.

We searched it in silence for a few minutes, until one of the other men found a piece of white card inside a polythene bag resting under a tiny cairn of stones. It said: *Augustin's*, and was followed by another grid reference. We consulted the map and found that it was not much further on.

The new site was inside a wood and we found it with comparative ease. It was made up of several tents of various sizes, ranging from crude sheets of canvas large enough to shelter only one or two persons, up to a medium-sized marquee of the sort once found at circuses. The whole encampment was fenced off, except at one place where a large tent had been erected. Anyone wishing to enter the encampment therefore had to pass through this tent.

Over the entrance was tacked a crudely painted sign on what had once been a sheet or tablecloth: AUGUSTIN. Underneath that was written: SCREW FOR PIECE. We went inside.

A young boy sat behind a trestle table.

I said to him, 'Is Augustin here?'

'He's busy.'

'Too busy to see us?'

'How many?'

I told the boy the number of men there were in our group. He left the tent and walked through into the encampment. A few minutes later Augustin himself joined us. Few refugees know what nationality Augustin is. He is not British.

He said to me, 'You got men?'

'Yes.'

'When they coming?'

I told him in about an hour. He looked at his watch.

'OK. But out by six?'

We agreed to this.

He added, 'We got more in evening. OK?'

We agreed again then returned to our own temporary camp where Rafiq and the others were waiting for us. It occurred to me that if we told the others the exact location of Augustin's, some of them would inevitably slip away and try to get there before the rest of us. An imagined freedom to pick and choose amongst the women was a priority for us all. I therefore would not divulge the exact location, even to Rafiq, but said only that Augustin's camp had moved from the last reference point. When it was clear I intended to say nothing more until we actually set out, we all settled down and ate some food. After we had eaten I led the others to Augustin's.

Rafiq went into the main tent with myself and the other two men. The remainder crushed in behind us, or waited outside. I noticed that while I had been away, Augustin had tidied up his own appearance and had placed a wooden barrier across the inner flap of the tent to prevent us from passing straight through.

He was sitting behind the trestle table. At his side was a tall white woman, with long black hair and remarkable blue eyes. She glared at us with what I took to be contempt.

Augustin said, 'How much you offer?'

'How much do you want?' Rafiq said.

'What you got?'

'Food.'

'No food.'

'Food is the best we can offer you.'

'No food. We want rifles. Or women.'

Rafiq said, 'We have fresh meat. And chocolate. And plenty of tinned fruit.'

Augustin tried to look displeased, but I could tell he was unable to resist accepting our offers.

'OK. Rifles?'

'No.'

'Women?'

Rafiq told him, without mentioning the abduction, that we had no women. Augustin spat on to the surface of the table.

'How many slaves?'

'We haven't got any.'

I expected Augustin not to believe this. Rafiq had told me that at his last visit, when Augustin was in a more expansive mood, he had confided that he 'knew' every group of white travellers took along African refugees as slaves or hostages. Setting the moral issue entirely aside, the sheer practical fact of the constant searches and interrogations by police and other forces would have made this impossible. It was self-evidently a fantasy. In any case, Augustin appeared to take our word for it.

'OK. What food?'

Rafiq passed him a sheet of paper, containing a list of

provisions which we would be willing to hand over. The woman read it out to him.

'No meat. We have enough. It stink too quick. More chocolate. Canned food.'

Finally, the barter was agreed. Knowing what had had to be paid in the past, I realized that Rafiq had struck a bargain. Either that, or Augustin's business was not as good as it had been. I had expected the price to be higher. But I did wonder about his insistence on weapons.

We moved outside the tent to our handcarts and off-loaded the agreed amounts of food. The business side accomplished, we were conducted through the tent and into a small clearing.

Augustin was standing with three of his whores. I stepped forward before any of the other men and chose the woman standing closest to me. She was tall, full-breasted and wide-hipped. I guessed her age to be about twenty-five. As I spoke to her she bared her teeth as if I were to inspect those, too.

She led me away from the clearing to a small tent at the very edge of the encampment. There was little room inside the tent, so she took off her clothes outside. As she did so, I looked round at the other tents. I could see that outside each one the other women were also undressing.

When she was naked she went inside. I took off my trousers and laid them on the ground next to where she had put her clothes. I followed her inside.

She was lying on a rough bed made out of several old blankets thrown on the ground. There were no flaps at either end of the tent and had she been even a little taller both her head and her feet would have stuck out. I entered the tent and crawled in between her legs and lay down on top of her. As I entered her there was no particular sensation of flesh meeting flesh – instead, I was distracted by a cold hardness of metal by her side. It had a sharp edge. At first all I wanted to do was move the thing out of the way, because it was pressing against me, but when I touched it I realized that what I could feel was the trigger and guard of a rifle.

As we fucked I managed to push the rifle away from us and towards the edge of the tent. The woman, whose eyes were closed, and who was responding physically to my sex, gave no sign of being aware of what I was doing. In a few moments I had managed to slide the rifle away from us, although it was still partly covered by the blankets.

My preoccupation with the presence of the weapon had lessened my sexual desire and I found that my erection was softening, even though I had continued to make movements against her. I returned my attention to the woman and her body – I was aroused by her again. Her aromas rose excitingly around me. But because of what had happened I took much longer than normal to come to a climax, and by the time I finished we were both sweaty.

Afterwards we dressed and returned to the clearing. The other men made ribald comments about how long I had taken. The woman I had been with lined up with the others again, and immediately another man went to her.

As they headed towards the tents I stepped past the others, through the tent with the trestle-table where Augustin and his woman sat with a pile of the provisions we had bartered, and out to where we had left the handcarts.

I walked past them into the trees.

I turned and looked back. Augustin was watching me suspiciously from the entrance to his tent. I made a lewd gesture towards my crutch, indicating that I was about to urinate, and he waved to me. I walked on.

When I was out of sight of the encampment I turned and walked in a broad circle, keeping the camp on my left.

After a while I turned in towards it again and approached it cautiously. I came to the camp from the side. No one saw me.

Using every available tree and bush as cover, I moved around until I was opposite the tent where I had been. Again making sure that I was not observed I crawled up to it on my hands and knees. I lay beside it on my stomach, the boundary rope directly above me.

Inside, the man was insulting the whore, cursing and blaspheming and insulting her race. His voice was rasping and high-pitched with excitement. She replied, groaning passionately.

I slid my hand under the flap of the tent, found the rifle and gripped it. With a slowness that nearly panicked me I slid it out from under the blankets, then beneath the loose edge of the tent. I made for the cover of the trees. I secreted the rifle in the wildly growing brambles of a hawthorn bush, before walking back to the camp.

As I went past Augustin he made a vulgar comment about urine. He was eating some of the chocolate and had brown smudges around his mouth.

When the college closed I found myself in the second major financial crisis of my life. For a while Isobel and I carried on by drawing out our savings, but within a month I knew I would have to find some other kind of job. I kept hearing that the college was about to reopen, which made me delay any decisions. I telephoned the administrative section of the college on several occasions, but I was rarely able even to obtain an answer. In the meantime I looked around in a half-hearted way for another job.

The country was in deep recession. We had a government that prided itself on fiscal expertise, but they made one bad

74

decision after another. John Tregarth and his government had first come to power because of their economic policies but the balance of payments was in the red for month after month, public borrowing was at an all-time high, prices continued to rise steeply and an increasing number of people were made unemployed. At first, confident of myself and my Master's Degree in English History, I toured the offices of publishers intending to pick up some temporary position as an editor or adviser. I was soon disabused of the illusion about the supposed value of such a degree, finding that the world of books, like virtually everything else, was cutting back on expense and staff at every opportunity. With a similarly universal sequence of sadly shaking heads, I found that the way into some form of clerical work was also barred. Manual labour was, by and large, out of the question. Since the middle seventies the industrial labour-pool had been directed by the unions. In most established companies a closed shop was in operation, and where there was not, and the labour was casual and therefore underpaid, every available job was filled from the huge numbers of immigrants.

At this stage I became deeply depressed and approached my father for assistance. Although he was now retired he had been managing director of a small chain of companies and still had some influence. Going to my father was close to a last resort. Neither of us liked the brief contact into which this brought us, as we had hardly communicated at all for several years. Reluctantly, and with bad grace on both sides, he managed to obtain me an insignificant position in a cloth-cutting factory. It saved me. I never found a way to express my gratitude to him, nor the regrets that grew about the way we had treated each other for so long. He died a few months later, but he still knew nothing about my change of heart.

With my immediate money problems solved, I started to pay attention again to what was going on in the country. There was no sign of any improvement, and in many respects things were growing steadily worse. What I had always thought of as normal was long gone. Every small feature of life became an issue of some kind: travelling around, what they showed on television (or in many cases did not show), the price of food in the shops, the increase in violent crimes, children having to share places at school, waiting lists of two or three years at hospitals, a steadily increasing number of power-outs and gas shortages.

There were also larger, more general problems. It turned out that the closing of the college was part of a scheme introduced covertly by the Ministry of Education to reduce the number of places available for higher education. The main universities were for the time being secure, but in every town and city many centres of adult education, or places offering vocational courses, or the skills-based polytechnics, were closing. Six months after I lost my teaching job, the old college buildings had been converted to commercial premises, and the grounds sold to property developers. Nor was the government carrying out this plan against public opinion: to many people the universities were thought to be the foundation of the liberal outlook that had created the mess in the first place. There was at first something of a public outcry when the closures first became widely known, but popular interest soon passed to other things.

The work I did at the cloth factory was menial and undemanding. I had to cut certain types and colours of cloth to determined lengths, ensure that they were labelled and packed correctly, and follow through each consignment to the despatch point. I had to do this a dozen times a day, more in busy periods. Within a week I had learned everything I

needed to know about the work and from there it degenerated into a meaningless routine which I acted out for the
sole purpose of the money it brought me.

I said to Isobel, 'We need to talk. Come over here for a
minute.'

'I want to talk to you too.'

We left Sally by the tents and walked back to where I had
been before. We stood facing each other, awkward in each
other's presence. I realized that this was the first time I had
been really alone with her for several days, if not weeks. That
thought led me to remembering that we had not had sex for
over three months.

I tried not to look at her.

'Alan, we've got to do something,' she said. 'We can't
go on like this. I'm terrified of what's going to happen. We
ought to return to London. It isn't fair on Sally.'

'I don't know what to do,' I said. 'We can't go back, we
can't reach Bristol. All we can do is wait.'

'But wait for *what*?'

'How do I know? Until things settle down again. You
know the position as well as I do.'

'Have you thought what this is doing to Sally? Have you
looked at her recently? Have you thought about what this is
doing to me?'

'I know what it's doing to all of us.'

'And you do damn-all about it!'

'If you've got any positive suggestions –'

'Steal a car from someone. Shoot someone. Do *anything*,
but get us out of this damned field and back to decent living! There must be somewhere we can go. Things would be
all right at my parents' house. Or we could go back to that
camp. I'm sure they'd have us if they saw Sally.'

'What's wrong with Sally?'

'Nothing you'd ever notice.'

'What do you mean?'

She didn't answer, but I thought I caught her meaning. There was nothing wrong with Sally I didn't know about, but Isobel was using her against me.

I said, 'Be reasonable. You can't expect me to solve everything. There's nothing you or I can do. If there was, we'd do it.'

'There must be *something*. We can't live in a tent in somebody's field for ever.'

'Look, the country's in one hell of a state. I don't know what's going on, and I doubt if we would if we were in London. There are police on all the main roads, troops in most of the towns. There are no newspapers any more, and nothing on the radio. All I'm suggesting is that we wait this out as long as we have to, until things get better. Even if we had a car we probably wouldn't be able to drive it. How long is it since we saw one on the road?'

Isobel burst into tears. I tried to comfort her but she pushed me away. I stood by her, waiting for her to calm down. I was becoming confused. When I had thought about what I was going to say to her it had seemed to be so simple. As she wept, Isobel stepped away from me, shouldering me aside as I tried to pull her back. Across the field I could see Sally staring in our direction.

When Isobel had stopped crying, I said to her, 'What do you want most of all?'

'There's no point in telling you.'

'Yes, there is.'

She shrugged hopelessly. 'I think I want us to be as we were before this started.'

'Living in Southgate? With all those rows going on?'

She said, 'And you off with one of your women, out till all hours of the night.'

Isobel had known about my affairs. She no longer possessed the ability to sting me by accusing me of them. I had enough sting of self-remorse.

'You'd prefer that to this?' I said. 'Would you really? Think about it, will you?'

'I've thought about it,' she said.

'And about the rest of the marriage? Would you honestly want any of that back again?' I had already considered the question, knew my own answer to it. Our marriage had finished before it began.

'Anything ... rather than this.'

'That's no answer, Isobel.'

I debated again whether or not to say to her what I had decided. As callous as it seemed to me in the face of her present state of mind, it presented an alternative to a situation we both detested. Though she wanted to retrogress and I was going to move on. Was there, I wondered, any real significance?

'All right,' she said. 'How about this? We'll split up. You go back to London and try to find somewhere for us to live. I'll take Sally and we'll try to reach Bristol. We'll stay there until we hear from you.'

I said at once, 'No. Absolutely not. I'm not letting you take Sally. I don't trust you with her.'

'What do you mean? You don't trust me, her mother?'

'Being a mother doesn't embrace every capability.'

For a second or two I saw genuine hatred in Isobel's face and I looked away. My infidelity to Isobel in the past had been a reaction away from her, rather than some distinct move towards someone else I preferred. I was never looking for someone better. Everything I did had come about through my inadequacy to face up to our marriage, not out of awareness of some shortcomings in the relationship. Though I realized that our generally unsuccessful sex life, which I knew had begun with some inner difficulty Isobel was struggling with, was one of the first causes, it was no longer the whole reason. It was the complexity of our failure that made me unable to deal with it. My own motives were suspect. Thus, in provoking Isobel's overt hatred, I felt wrong and wronged all at once.

She said, 'That's what I want. You're obviously incapable of supplying an alternative.'

'I do have a suggestion.'

'What is it?'

And so I told her. I said I was taking Sally and that she was to go on to Bristol by herself. I offered her most of our remaining cash and as much food, camping equipment, and so on, as she wanted. When she asked me why I wished to do this, I told her. I said bluntly that it was obvious our marriage was over, that the social upheaval we had suffered had only shifted the nature of our problems. I told her that if she persisted in thinking that we could pick up again she was deluding herself and, in the long run, jeopardizing Sally's future. The break had been forced on us but nevertheless it was a natural one. I considered that Sally would be safer with me, and that when things settled down again we could obtain a divorce and Sally would get legal protection.

Isobel just said, 'I don't know,' and walked away.

I had a look the stolen rifle as soon as I could and discovered that it was one for which we were already carrying ammunition. Rafiq had charge of this so I had to tell him that I had the rifle.

Rafiq already had the ammunition when I first joined his group, so I had no idea how he had found it.

I had a quiet chat with him. He told me that he had twelve rounds of ammunition, but warned me that it was in the interests of us all to get rid of the weapon at once. When I asked him why, he simply asked me if I had heard that the death penalty had been reintroduced for the unlicensed use of firearms.

'There's no rule of law any more,' I said, but to be honest this information made me nervous.

'OK, but it means it's every man for himself from now on.'

'Then we're better off with a rifle than we are without,' I said.

'That all depends, Whitman,' Rafiq said, and unusually he looked me straight in the eye.

I concluded privately that what he really meant was that he was envious of my having found the rifle. I argued the need for protection, that had we been armed earlier we might have been able to protect the women. I pointed out that atrocities against refugees were on the increase, and that there was now no organized force which we could trust.

Rafiq pointed out the increased frequency of arrests and interrogations, and that so far we had managed to avoid personal violence against ourselves. He told me about other refugee groups which had suffered police beatings, and imprisonment, torture and rape at the hands of militias.

His contention was that we had largely avoided this because when anyone searched us it was obvious we were defenceless.

I told him that I was prepared to accept any and all consequences of my being found in possession of the rifle; that if we were taken for interrogation I would hide it at once, and that if I was caught actually holding or using the rifle I would absolve everyone else from any knowledge of it.

Rafiq said OK. He didn't act that way, though, and he held on to his ammunition for another day. In the end he passed it over to me.

I took the weapon to pieces, cleaned and lubricated it, and learned how to sight it. Unwilling to waste any of the ammunition, or to draw attention to ourselves by the sound of it, I did not fire it. A man in our group who knew something of rifles told me that it was powerful and accurate, and he asked me if I had been trained to use it.

In the days that followed I could sense that there had been a subtle shift of emphasis in the way in which the group organized itself.

I came to town in the early afternoon, while arrangements for the day's festivities were in their last stages. The square in the centre of the town had been cleared of cars and people walked across the open space as if unaware that on normal days the town was jammed tight with the traffic passing through towards the coast.

Most of the shops which opened on the square had laid out wooden stands in front of their windows and piled them with goods. Several men worked on the tops of ladders, attaching coloured bunting across the streets. Nearly every window ledge was decorated with a handful of flowers.

At the wide end of the square, in front of the council offices, there was a small fairground, consisting of a children's roundabout, a helter-skelter, a row of swing-boats and several prize booths.

As I waited outside my hotel, a large coach stopped in a nearby side street and about fifty or sixty passengers climbed out and trooped into a mock-Tudor restaurant on the far side of the square. I waited until the last one was inside, then walked in the opposite direction until I was out of the town centre and in residential side streets.

When I returned the festivities were in full swing.

I caught my first sight of the girl as she stood by a display of handbags outside a leather store. It was the fashion at that time for girls to wear clothes made of very light material and with skirts well above the knee. She was dressed in pale blue and wore her hair straight and long. To me she was very beautiful. As I crossed the square towards her she moved on and was lost in the crowds. I waited by the leather shop, hoping to catch another glimpse of her, but was not able to. After a few minutes I changed my position and stood in the narrow alley that ran between the shooting gallery and coconut shy.

I returned to my hotel after an hour and ordered some coffee. Later, I went back into the square and saw her profile against the side of one of the lorries that transported the fairground rides. She was walking at right angles to my line of sight, staring thoughtfully at the ground. She reached the steps outside the council offices and walked up them. At the top she turned and faced me. Across the square we gazed at one another. I walked towards her.

I reached the bottom of the steps and she turned and went into the building. Not liking to follow her, I went up to where she had been standing and stood facing into the building. Behind me, I heard a loud report and a scream, and the sound of several people shouting. I did not turn. For about two minutes the square was noisy with the sound of shouting and music. Finally, someone thought to turn off the music that was being relayed by tannoy into the square, and silence fell. Somewhere a woman was sobbing.

Only as the ambulance arrived did I turn to face the square

and saw that an accident had happened on the roundabout. A small child was trapped by its legs between the platform and the motor in the centre.

I waited for the child to be released. The ambulance men did not appear to know how to go about it. Finally, a fire-appliance drove up and three men using an electric saw cut through the wood of the platform and freed the child's legs. The child was unconscious. As the ambulance drove away, and the music started up again, I realized that the girl stood beside me. I held her hand and led her away from the centre into the streets along which I had walked earlier.

Her beauty took away from me my ability for glib conversation. I wanted to flatter her and impress her, but the appropriate words would not flow.

We returned to my hotel in the evening and I bought her dinner. When we had finished eating she became distracted and told me she had to leave. I saw her to the door of the hotel but she would not allow me to escort her any further. I went into the hotel lounge and watched television for the rest of the evening.

The following morning I purchased a newspaper and learned that the child had died on the way to hospital. I threw away the newspaper.

I had arranged to meet Isobel in the afternoon and had until then in which to pass the time. For most of the morning I watched the men dismantling the fairground machinery and loading it on the lorries. By midday the square had been emptied of equipment and the police were allowing normal traffic to pass through.

After luncheon in the hotel I borrowed a friend's motorcycle and took it out on to the main road. Half an hour later in a buoyant mood, I met Isobel. She was wearing the pale-blue dress again, as I had requested. Again we walked, this time leaving the town and finding several paths through the countryside. I wanted to make love to her, but she would not allow me to.

On our way back to the town we were caught unexpectedly in a summer shower. I had planned to entertain her with another dinner at the hotel but instead we hitched a ride back to her house. She would not let me go inside with her. Instead, I promised to return to the town during the following week. She agreed to see me then.

As I went into the foyer of the hotel one of the porters told me that the mother of the child had committed suicide in the afternoon. It had been she, according to the porter, who had encouraged the child to stand on the roundabout as it was moving. For a while we discussed the tragedy, then I had a meal in the hotel restaurant. Afterwards I went to the local cinema where they were showing a double feature horror programme. In the interval between the first film and the second I noticed Isobel sitting a few rows in front of me, kissing a man who looked several years older than her. She didn't see me. I left at once and in the morning I returned to London.

In one village I discovered a radio. Its batteries were flat. I took them out of the back of the radio and warmed them slowly the next time I was near a fire. While they were still warm I put them back into the radio and switched it on.

At that time the BBC was broadcasting on one wavelength only, interspersing long sessions of light music with news reports. Though I listened until the batteries went flat two hours later, I heard no bulletin about the fighting, nor about the plight of the refugees, nor about any political subject whatsoever. I learned that there had been a plane crash in South America.

The next time I had batteries for the radio the only channel I could find was Radio Peace ... broadcast from a converted iron-ore ship moored off the Isle of Wight. The output of that was limited to prolonged prayer sessions, Bible readings and hymns.

We were running short of food again and Rafiq made the decision to approach the nearest village and arrange a barter. We consulted our maps.

From experience we had learned that it was good general policy to avoid any village or town with more than about a thousand inhabitants, or situated anywhere near a major road. We had found that many of such places were either occupied by one faction or another and were subject to martial law in practice as well as theory, or else that a small garrison or camp would be maintained. As this described most of the towns and villages we passed we had to obtain the bulk of our supplies from isolated hamlets and solitary farms and houses. If we were fortunate enough to find some-where that would provide us readily with what we needed, then we would either make camp nearby, or keep on the move in the immediate area.

Looking at the map, Rafiq made a decision to go towards a village about an hour's walk to the west of us. One of the other men dissented, saying that he had heard before joining Rafiq's band that beyond this village was a Nationalist Forces headquarters. He said he would be happier if we detoured around the town either through villages to the north or to the south.

For a while we discussed it, but finally Rafiq overruled us. He said that our primary concern was food and that because of the number of farms near the village we would stand the best chance of getting provisions there. As we approached the village we saw two or three farms securely barricaded and defended.

By an unwritten law of the countryside, refugees were allowed to traverse or camp in fields lying fallow, on condition they stole no food or attempted to enter the farmhouses. In all my time on the road, I was aware of this rule and like everyone else I tried to work within it.

A few weeks earlier some refugees from East Anglia had joined Rafiq's group, but they clearly adopted the attitude of every man for himself and Rafiq had separated us from them.

We passed the farmhouses, therefore, and headed for the village. As was our custom, Rafiq walked at the head of our column with three other men. Immediately behind them came the handcarts containing our possessions, camping equipment and goods for barter, and the rest of the group followed on behind.

Because of my rifle Rafiq told me to walk alongside the leading cart, secreting the weapon in the false bottom in which we normally concealed unacceptable materials during searches or interrogations.

By this I could sense there was a change in Rafiq's attitude towards the rifle. Whereas before he had maintained that it was better to be unarmed as a form of self-protection, I saw now that he acknowledged the need to defend ourselves even if that defence was not itself apparent to potential aggressors.

We came to the village along a minor road that ran across country from the town on the far side. Later it joined a major road further to the east of us. Again, it was from experience that we knew it was better to come to a strange village along a road rather than across the fields. Though we felt immediately more exposed, we believed we were establishing a better basis for the coming barter.

According to the map the village had no actual nucleus, but was more a straggling collection of houses along two narrow roads: the one we were on and one that crossed it at right angles. We passed the first house in silence. It had been abandoned and its windows were all broken. The same was true of the next house and the one after, and of all the houses we passed on our way to the centre.

As we rounded the bend, there was the sound of a shot in front of us and one of the men at Rafiq's side was thrown backwards.

We stopped. Those near the handcarts crouched down behind them, the others took what cover they could find at the side of the road. I looked down at the man who had fallen. He was on the ground an arm's length from where I crouched. The bullet had struck him in the throat, tearing away a large chunk of his neck. Blood spurted horribly from him and although his eyes stared skywards with the dull glaze of death, he continued to make faint rasping noises from what was left of his throat. In seconds, he quietened. I was utterly appalled by this. Although I had seen many dead bodies as we moved about the broken countryside, I had never actually been there as someone I knew died beside me.

I squirmed away from him, taking shelter on the other side of the handcart.

Ahead of us a barricade had been erected across the road. It wasn't the kind of barricade we were used to seeing – an untidy barrier of paving-stones, old cars or masonry – but had been designed purposefully and built with bricks and cement. In the centre was a narrow gate through which pedestrians could pass, and on either side of this were two protective raised sections behind which I could just make out the figures of men. As I watched one of them fired again and the bullet smashed into the wood of the front of the handcart not an arm's length from where I was. I crouched down even lower.

'Whitman! You've got the rifle. Shoot back.'

I looked over at Rafiq. He was lying on the ground with two other men, trying to shelter behind a low mound of earth.

I said, 'They're too well protected.'

I saw that the houses to each side of the barricade had been similarly defended with a wall of concrete. I wondered whether it would be possible to enter the village by going across the fields and coming to it from the side, but the inhabitants were so obviously hostile that there would be little point.

Reaching into the false bottom of the handcart I slid out the rifle and loaded it. I was aware that every member of our group was watching me. Still attempting to keep as close to the side of the cart as possible, I aimed the rifle towards the barricade, trying to find a target I would be reasonably certain of striking.

I waited for a movement.

In the next few seconds a variety of thoughts passed through my mind. This wasn't the first occasion on which I had been in possession of a lethal weapon, but it was the first time I had ever taken deliberate aim with the knowledge that if I was successful I would kill or injure somebody.

Rafiq said quietly, 'What are you waiting for?'

'I can't see anyone to aim at.'

'Put a shot over their heads. No ... wait. Let me think.'

I let the barrel sink. I had not wanted to fire. As the next few seconds passed I knew I would not be able to fire it in this premeditated way. Therefore, when Rafiq told me to return it to its hiding-place, I felt relieved. A direct order from him to shoot would have created an almost impossible situation for me.

'It's no good,' he said, not just to me, but to everyone in earshot. 'We'll never get in there. We'll have to retreat.'

I think I had known that from the moment of the first shot. I realized that to Rafiq this decision must mean a lot as it was in some ways a serious undermining of his authority. The man who had told Rafiq about the Nationalist garrison was near him but he said nothing.

There was a white sheet over the top of the handcart. We had used it on several occasions in the past when wishing to underline our neutrality. Rafiq asked me to pass it to him. He stood up, unfolding the cloth as he did so. No one at the barricade fired. I had to admire his bravery. Under the same circumstances of leadership I would have risked anyone's life but my own. When I am in danger I have found that my capacity for self-honesty overrules all my thoughts.

After several seconds Rafiq told us to get back in the road and to move away slowly. I stood up myself, crouching down behind the bulk of the handcart. Our little convoy began to move back the way we had come.

Rafiq stood between us and the hostile village. He held the white sheet at arm's length, as if to provide cover for the rest of us. Slowly, carefully, he stepped backwards, obviously uncertain what would happen if he turned and walked with the rest of us.

The handcart was halfway round the bend that would take us out of the line of fire, when the last shot sounded. Although some of the men not actually hauling on a hand-cart scattered to the sides of the road, the rest of us broke into a sprint until we were round the curve in the road. When we were all out of the line of gunfire we stopped.

Rafiq rejoined us a few seconds later. He was swearing violently. The bullet had passed through the white sheet and scuffed his sleeve. A piece of cloth the size of a saucer had been torn away from near his elbow. We realized that had the bullet been marginally higher it would have smashed his bone.

When I was in my sleeping bag that night I knew that Rafiq had come out of the day's events in a stronger position. I was glad that my own thoughts were private, for they revealed me to be a greater coward than I had feared. For the first time since she had been taken by the Afrims I felt a strong sexual urge for Isobel, missing and wanting her, tormented by false memories of happiness together.

In the afternoon I spent about an hour with Sally while Isobel walked into the village ahead of us, to try to obtain food. Money was now our most serious problem, as we had only a pound or two left out of all that we had brought with us.

In talking to Sally I found myself treating her as an adult for the first time. I knew that Isobel had not told her what she and I had discussed, and I certainly had not, but something must have communicated itself to her. Sally spoke and acted with what I felt was a suddenly increased sense of responsibility. This pleased me more than I could say.

The evening passed mostly in silence; certainly, Isobel and I only spoke once or twice, and then about practical matters. When night came we laid out in our tents in the manner we had done since the start: Isobel and Sally in one tent and myself in the other. I was regretting that the conversation with Isobel had not come to a more definite conclusion. As it was, I still felt nothing had been achieved.

91

I lay awake for an hour, then drifted into sleep. Almost at once, it seemed, I was awoken by Isobel.

I reached out and touched her; she was naked.

I said, 'What ...?'

'Sshh. You'll wake Sally.' She undid the zip of my sleeping-bag and lay down with her body against me. I put my arms around her and, still half asleep and unthinking of what had gone between us during the day, I began to caress her sexually.

Our love-making was not well matched. I was still half asleep, and Isobel was confusing me. I had not expected this at all. I could not concentrate and achieved orgasm only after a long time. Isobel, though, was voracious in a way I had never known her before, the noise of her gasps almost deafening me. She came to orgasm twice, disconcertingly violently the first time.

We lay together linked for several minutes afterwards, then Isobel murmured something and attempted to wriggle out from under me. I rolled to one side and she pulled away. I tried to restrain her, placing an arm around her shoulders. She said nothing, but clambered to her feet and went out of the tent. I lay back in the residual warmth of our bodies and fell asleep again.

In the morning Sally and I discovered Isobel had gone, and we were on our own.

There was a policy discussion the next day, stemming mainly from our lack of food. After checking our stores carefully we calculated that there was now only enough food to last us another two days. After that, we would have to get by on a diet of biscuits, chocolate and so forth, but of course that would only last a few days and was impossible in the long term.

This was our first real prospect of starvation, and none of us liked it.

Rafiq outlined the alternatives open to us.

He said that we could continue as we had been doing so far: moving from village to village, bartering for food as necessary, and pilfering exchangeable goods from abandoned buildings and cars as we came across them. He pointed out that the military activity around us was on the increase, and although because of our vagrancy we were not involved in it, we could not afford to ignore it. People still living in towns and villages were taking defensive precautions accordingly. Everyone was suspicious of us.

Rafiq recounted to us a story he had not previously told, about a village he knew of in the north of England. This had been taken over by a group of African refugees claiming to be a part of the regular Afrim forces. They were wearing fatigues and battle gear, but no one had been able to identify which unit they were from, if any. Although the Africans had not established a proper garrison, and appeared to have no military discipline, the suspicions of the villagers were not aroused. After the first week, when suddenly rumours went round that units of the Nationalist Army were in the neighbourhood, the Africans had run amok, killing many dozens of civilians before the Nationalist forces arrived.

This, Rafiq said, was not an isolated incident. Similar outrages had been recorded all over the country and had been committed by members of the armed forces on all three sides of the conflict. From the point of view of the ordinary citizens, all outsiders were best treated as enemies. This attitude was spreading, he said, and made more hazardous our attempts to trade with civilians.

Another alternative would be to surrender ourselves formally to one side or another and then, almost certainly as a consequence, enrol into the military. The arguments for this were strong: it would give a shape and purpose to the kind of life we were already having to lead, the fact we were all reasonably healthy men capable of military duty, and finally it would commit us to a situation that we were already deeply involved with.

We could join the Nationalists, the so-called 'legal' army that defended the policies of Tregarth's government, but one that was now apparently carrying out a policy of genocide against the immigrants. We could join the Royal Secessionists, the white supporters of the Afrim cause who although officially non-legal and under continuous sentence of death by the Tregarth régime, had much public support in some quarters. If Tregarth's government were to be over-thrown, either from within by a military coup or by effective diplomatic action from the UN, it was probable that the Secessionists would take or sponsor office. We could join the United Nations peace-keeping force, which although technically non-participating, in effect had had to intervene militarily on many occasions. Or we could align ourselves with one of the outside participants, such as the US Marine Corps (which had taken over civilian police responsibility) or the theoretically uncommitted Commonwealth forces, who had little effect on the progress of the war beyond further confusing the situation.

Another choice open to us, Rafiq said, was to surrender ourselves to a civilian welfare organization and move towards official refugee status within some kind of quasi-legal situation. Though this was superficially an attractive alternative, it was doubtful if any of us would be taking it in practice. Until the military situation quietened down, and the social effects of the Afrim uprising were absorbed, such a recourse would be hazardous. In any event, it would mean ultimately that we would have to live under Tregarth's government, which would automatically involve us again in the crisis in the cities and with the displacement of people from their houses. This was continuing.

Rafiq said that it was our present lack of effective involvement which was the best argument for continuing to stay as we were. In any event, the main drive of most of the men was to locate and be reunited with their women. Surrendering ourselves to one or another of the participating factions would lessen our chances of this.

A vote was taken and we elected to do as Rafiq suggested. We carried on towards the next village, probably an hour or two to the north of us.

Again I detected a feeling amongst the other men that Rafiq's position had been strengthened both by the shooting at the barricade the day before, and by his reasoned arguing of the alternatives. I myself had no wish to become involved with him in a struggle for power, but nevertheless my possession of the rifle could not be entirely ignored by him.

As we moved northwards I walked at his side.

By this time I had bought my own motorcycle and used it on those weekends when I went to see Isobel.

My early days of recklessness had passed and though I still enjoyed the sensation of speed, I kept to within the legal limits for much of the time. It was rare for me, when by myself, to open up the cycle and take it to its maximum speed, though when Isobel was on the back she often encouraged me to drive faster.

Our relationship was developing more slowly than I would have liked.

Before I had met her I had enjoyed several physical affairs

with other girls, and though Isobel could present me with no moral, religious or physical reason why we should not sleep together, she had never allowed me to go further than superficial contact. I persevered, wanting to enjoy a more mature physical friendship.

One afternoon we rode on the motorbike up to a hill a long distance from where she was living, where there was a gliding club. We watched the sailplanes overhead for a while, but soon grew bored.

On our ride back to town, Isobel nudged me from behind, shouted in my ear, and directed me away from the road and into a copse of trees. We went a long way into the woodland, off the paths, the road no longer visible nor its traffic audible. Green peacefulness surrounded us. We dismounted the motorbike, sat together on the grass and twigs, held hands and kissed. This time, it was she who made all the moves, kissing me with an energy and affection she had never shown before. She did not stop me when I undid the buttons on her blouse and ran my hand over her breasts. The moment, though, my hand went inside her bra and touched her nipple, she pulled away from me. But she had led me too far and I didn't want to stop. I fought against her, pulling eagerly at her clothes. She kept trying to stop me, but in the struggle I managed to tear off her bra and skirt, ripping the skirt, and also pulled her pants halfway down her thighs.

Then I realized what was happening, that she genuinely wanted me to stop, and I backed off. We lay side by side on the rough ground of the woodland, Isobel weeping, while I fought to calm myself. I was coursing with sexual desire for her, felt more excitement than I had ever known before, yet I was also confused and hurt by the contradictions in what she seemed to want and what she was prepared to do.

A long time passed with nothing said. Isobel covered up

what she could of her body, but her skirt was ruined. She wrapped it around herself, then sat down on the pillion of the bike and waited for me to take her home. I drove her slowly to her parents' house, and she went inside without speaking to me. I returned to my room at the hall of residence that evening and did not see her again for more than three weeks.

The news from Africa began to dominate the newspaper headlines and television bulletins, but for a long time most people thought of it as another distant war, trouble elsewhere. The media speculated endlessly about the impact it might have on countries in the West, but it continued to seem remote from our daily lives. Most of the concern being expressed was over the likely interruption to supplies of crude oil from the Nigerian basin.

The disputes were complex and far-reaching. Food resources were a major part of the problem. The Sahel underwent several consecutive years of drought. The Upper Nile became polluted. Large areas of sub-Saharan Africa were suffering famine. There were many countries which had been taken over by military force, which now seemed intent on exterminating each other. Mineral resources became disputed: the oil in Nigeria, the uranium and copper in the Congo, the gold and diamonds in South Africa. Water rights were disputed everywhere, with claims that rivers were being diverted or dammed. Ancient tribal disputes were flaring up, deeply complicated by the emergence of Christian and Muslim fundamentalism. There were several reports of genocide. And perhaps the most dangerous element: the weapons trade, selling all manner of weapons to almost anyone who could pay for them. The five richest nations on the continent were soon nuclear-capable, and several other areas or racial groups formed alliances with nuclear powers in other parts of the world.

At this time I was still lecturing at the college in North London. Gradually, inexorably, the subjects I was trying to teach turned to these problems. I discovered that I was fielding questions from the students every day about history, politics, nuclear disarmament, ecology.

I tried to keep abreast of what was happening but it was almost impossible to find reliable news. Large areas of the continent were either forbidden to foreign journalists and diplomats, or else they were so dangerous that no one could go there. Elsewhere, the media were heavily censored or administered. And the disputes were fast-moving, a series of alliances, betrayals, accusations, swift military occupations and the inevitable consequences for the civilian population of displacement, starvation and disease.

I had grown up during the years of the Cold War between NATO and the Soviet Union, with a kind of background fear throughout my youth that an unimaginable nuclear holocaust could be unleashed at any moment. My students had the same fears, but because many of them came from African countries they had a more sharply focused fearfulness. When it came to it, the holocaust was the not one I had feared, but the one they had been dreading. The bombing of African states by other African states was over in a matter of days. There was one wave of rocket-launched attacks, then four days later a round of retaliations. It ceased after that. Nuclear wars, it seemed, were soon over.

Contact was lost with most parts of the continent. Humanitarian aid was sent, arrived, but distribution or administration was almost impossible. Parts of the continent were relatively untouched, so brave intentions were announced, but the reality of gaining access to the rest of the interior was a complex problem. There were no communications, no roads or airfields known to be open, no infrastructure had survived that was usable, and whole regions had become wastelands of radioactive debris. Large areas of the forested central zone were blazing and continued to blaze for more than a year. A girdle of smoke and fall-out spread around the globe. No one knew how many people had been killed. No one knew how many survivors there were, or in what sort of physical condition they were. The necessity for humanitarian relief became the prime global concern.

The people of Britain, sufficiently far away to be safe from any direct threat, did what they could. They contributed generously to relief funds. They volunteered to take part in aid initiatives. Truck convoys of relief supplies set off. People said and did little in public, but in private it was clear everyone was obsessed and upset by the disaster. Of course, no one was totally isolated from the tragedy: most people had friends or relatives or business associates or acquaintances who had probably been caught up in the catastrophe. Gaining information about individuals who had been in Africa during the war was impossible. Africa had become a silent, smouldering, smoking wasteland. Above and below every feeling was the knowledge that it was in our lifetimes that the most catastrophic war in history had been fought.

Meanwhile, democracy was taking its turn, and a General Election was held in Britain. It was a time of economic recession, with many people jobless. Inflation was high, loans were difficult to obtain, many companies were going out of business. A new right-wing party, initially a splinter group from the Conservatives, campaigned successfully on the basis of economic reform and isolationism as a cure for our employment problems. The UK Reform Party, under the leadership of John Tregarth, gained power with a tiny majority. The African catastrophe occurred four months into the first term of office under Reform. When the scale of the disaster was clear, and the possible future impact it might have on lives in Britain, Tregarth called a snap election. This time the message from the Reform party was protectionism, security of borders, precautions against epidemics, anti-immigration, everything short of overt racism. Tregarth was re-elected with a substantial majority.

Aid agencies finally managed to penetrate the areas of Africa worst affected by the bombing. Most major cities had been destroyed and large areas of open land had been blasted or burned. Casualties were incalculable. There was hardly a gleam of hope at first – endless reports came back from Africa describing the horrors of the destruction and its thermonuclear aftermath.

Such was the devastation and loss of life that it was impossible to conceive of a worse situation. But then one emerged, and it was one that Tregarth had somehow foreseen. There were survivors. Not everywhere had been struck directly by nuclear warheads, not everyone had been killed in the first detonations. Some people had survived the bombing. Many were to die later from the results of flash burns, radiation sickness and the residual radioactivity, but most did not and they survived. They were sick, thirsty and hungry, but they were alive. At first there appeared to be only a handful of these people, but the immensity and topographical complexity of the continent meant that as the weeks went by an increasing number of people straggled out of the undamaged zones, seeking help. Soon there were thousands of them, then hundreds of thousands. Finally there were millions. Nearly all were homeless, none had food, fresh water, medical care.

It was a second disaster unprecedented in history

The relief agencies were entirely incapable of dealing with the survivors. Money and resources poured in from all over the world, but the sheer scale of the problem was beyond the capability of the workers to give even the most basic aid.

People continued to die, not only of starvation, of thirst, of radiation sickness, but also of the traditional diseases of privation: cholera, dysentery, typhoid, tuberculosis.

The months went by without improvement. It was clear to everyone, victims and workers alike, that continental Africa was no longer capable of supporting human life. While the refugee camps continued to fill up, and the aid workers struggled to cope, so there developed a drift away towards the coasts.

The people fled. The leaving began slowly but within three months it had built into a rush. Before the first anniversary of the war it had turned into an exodus. Any boat or aircraft that could be found and made to operate was used. The emigrants headed for anywhere that was away from Africa.

They landed in due course in countries all over the world: India, France, Turkey, the Middle East, the USA, Greece, Australia, the Soviet Union. During this period of mass evacuation, it was estimated that between seventeen and twenty million people abandoned Africa in search of safety. In the course of about a year, just over two million of them found their way to Britain and landed there.

The Africans, the Afrims, were welcome nowhere. But where they landed they stayed. In most countries, gradually, awkwardly, the long slow process of asylum and assimilation began. Everywhere there was social upheaval, but in Britain, where the country had installed a neo-racist government without realizing how the world would change, they did much worse.

*

I reported to the recruiting station at the appointed time of one-thirty in the afternoon.

For several days there had been a saturation of advertisements on television and in the press, stating that entry into the armed forces was still voluntary, but that conscription was to be introduced in the next few weeks. This statement was underlined with an implication that men who volunteered straight away would be given preferential treatment over those who were eventually drafted.

I learned through friends of mine that certain categories of men would be the first to be called up. My new job at the cloth factory qualified me for one of these categories, while had I still been employed as an academic I would have been in the protected category.

I was not happy at the factory and the pay in the army would be much higher. I therefore had more than one motive when I reported for the medical examination.

I had applied for officer training, learning from the advertisements that a degree was sufficient to establish suitability. I was directed to a specific room in the building where a sergeant major in dress uniform told me what to do, adding the word 'sir' to the end of every sentence.

I was given an IQ test, which was marked in my presence. The errors I made were carefully explained to me. Then I was questioned sketchily on my background and political standing, and finally I was instructed to remove my clothes and to go to the next room.

The lighting was bright. There was a wooden bench along one wall and I was told to sit on it while waiting for the doctor. I was the only person there. A long time passed without anything happening. The room was not cold, but because I was naked in a strange place I felt exceptionally vulnerable and chilled.

I had been waiting for fifteen minutes when a young female nurse came in and sat at a desk immediately opposite to where I was sitting. I was embarrassed to be naked in front of her like this, entirely exposed to her gaze. My arms were folded across my chest and not liking to attract her attention by moving them I stayed still. I crossed my legs in an attempt to conceal myself.

I was in a position of exceptional sexual vulnerability, and although she paid hardly any attention to me, and I told myself that as a professional she would be used to seeing men in the nude, I was constantly aware of her presence. She was dark and pretty, and I sensed that she could not be completely unaware of me. I saw a light smile once, as she turned her head to reach for another file. I felt a tightening in my groin, and to my consternation realized that my penis was beginning to erect.

Awareness of the tumescence did nothing to reduce the condition. I tried to restrain the organ by gripping it tightly between my thighs, but this soon became painful. It was at this point that the nurse glanced up from her work and looked at me. As she did so, the penis swung out of the restraint of my legs and assumed its fully erect position. I covered it at once with my hands. The nurse looked back at her work.

'The doctor will see you in a few moments,' she said.

I sat motionlessly, concealing my penis with my hands. I watched the clock on the wall and three more minutes passed. I still had a full erection when a man in a white coat appeared at the far end of the room and asked me to step inside. As it would have appeared unnatural to walk across the room with my hands at my crutch, I reluctantly allowed my arms to swing at my side. I was aware of the nurse's gaze on my body as I walked past her desk.

Once I was inside the examination room the erection began to dwindle and in less than a minute had gone altogether.

I was given a routine medical check-up, had my chest X-rayed and samples of my blood and urine taken. I was presented with a form to sign which stated that subject only to medical suitability I would be commissioned into the British Nationalist Army as a trainee 2nd Lieutenant, and that I would report for duty at the time and place indicated on my mobilization certificate. I signed it and was handed my clothes again.

There followed an interview with a man in civilian clothing, who questioned me at great length on subjects central to my overall character and personality. It was a difficult interview and I was glad when it was over. I know that during it I revealed my brief membership in the pro-Afrim society at the college, and this made him ask many questions about my motives and political beliefs..

A week later I received a duplicated letter which stated that my medical examination had revealed a liver complaint and that my temporary commission was therefore terminated.

The day before this letter arrived conscription was re-introduced by the Ministry of Internal Security, which coincided with an increase in militant Afrim activities. A month later, with the massacre of the Nationalist troops at Colchester barracks and the arrival of the first American aircraft carrier in the Irish Sea, I realized that the military situation was more serious than I had imagined. Though relieved at my own lack of personal involvement, day-to-day life became increasingly difficult and my own experiences as a civilian were not much easier than anyone else's.

After receiving the letter from the military I visited my own doctor. He investigated the complaint in my liver and then referred me to a consultant. I underwent a series of intensive and painful tests. A few days later I was informed by letter that there was nothing wrong with my liver.

We encountered a large band of Africans and were at once uncertain of what was to happen. We had the choice of three courses of action: run from them, show our defensive ability with the rifle or meet them.

What worried us most was that they were not wearing recognizable Afrim uniforms, but were clad in the same sort of clothes as ourselves. It was possible that they were a group of civilian refugees, but we had heard that Nationalist troops treated such people extremely badly if they came across them. As a result most African refugees had surrendered themselves to the welfare organizations. The few who remained had integrated themselves with sympathetic white groups if they could find them.

The men we met were friendly, well-fed and appeared to be unarmed. They did have three large handcarts near to which we were not allowed to approach. It seemed likely to both me and Rafiq that there were weapons concealed inside them.

We spoke for several minutes, exchanging the usual pieces of news which were the only real currency on the refugee network. The men showed no signs of nerves, nor any awareness that we ourselves were in an edgy state.

They did however reveal certain signs of excitement, but we had no idea why. Our main concern during the meeting was for our own safety. In the end we moved on, leaving the men near a wood. We crossed a field, then passed out of sight.

Rafiq called me over to him.

'They were Afrim guerrillas,' he said. 'Did you notice their identity-bracelets?'

Sally and I waited for a few hours to see whether Isobel was going to return. I felt unable to explain to Sally why she had left us. It was difficult even to account for it to myself. Which of us was most to blame? I asked myself, and so on. I worked out from Sally's manner that she had been expecting something terrible to happen between her parents and I suspected that she probably saw herself to blame for it. I tried to reassure her about that, and minimized the upset I was feeling myself, but having an adult conversation to explain what had happened was beyond me. All I could think was that she did seem to be accepting the new situation.

Isobel had taken with her exactly half of our remaining money, in addition to a suitcase of her own clothes and some of the food. She had left all the camping and sleeping equipment with us.

By midday it was obvious that Isobel was not coming back. I began to make preparations for a meal, but Sally said she would do it. I allowed her to take over and meanwhile packed our gear. At this point I had made no decision about what we were to do, but I felt that it was time to leave this particular location.

When we had eaten, I set out for Sally as best I could what I thought our options might be.

My main feeling at this time was a sense of demoralization and inadequacy. For everything that had been going wrong between Isobel and me, I had not expected her to walk out on me. I tried to conceal this from Sally. I explained to her that her mother and I had agreed that we were to return to London, while she went on to Bristol. We were not going to return to our house but we were going to find somewhere

106

new to live. Sally told me that she understood, but she asked several questions about her friends and which school she would have to go to.

I then tried to describe for her some of the difficulties facing us. I said we no longer knew what was going on in the country and that we could trust no one. I told her we had very little money, that it would not be possible to go back by car, and that we would probably have to hike for the major part of the way.

Sally said, 'But couldn't we go on a train, Daddy?'

Children have a facility for cutting sideways across a problem and seeing obvious solutions that have eluded their parents. In all the time we had been living rough in the countryside I had completely forgotten the existence of the railway system. I wondered if Isobel had similarly not thought of it, or whether she was intending to reach Bristol that way.

'It could be a question of money,' I replied. 'We might not have enough. We'll have to find out. Is that what you'd like to do?'

'Yes. I don't want to live in the tent any more.'

I had learned that it was not possible to plan too far ahead, but I couldn't avoid worrying about what we would do if the situation in London was as bad as when we had left. If the forceful occupation of houses by militant Afrims was continuing, and the law-enforcement agencies were as divided in London as we had seen in the countryside, then we would be among thousands of other people looking for accommodation. If the situation was as bad as I feared, we might have to leave London once more. If that happened then the only place I could think of going to was my younger brother's house in Carlisle. Even if we were able to travel safely that far I was not at all sure what kind of reception we would receive. I could see no alternative. Edward was the only remaining member of my family after the death of my parents four years before, and of Clive, my elder brother, in the confrontation at Bradford. But Edward and I had parted bitterly. I had managed to alienate most of my family.

As far as Sally was concerned, though, the matter was settled. We collected the remainder of our belongings and packed them. I carried our suitcase and the rucksack, and Sally carried the other bag containing our clothes. We walked eastwards, not knowing the location of the nearest railway station, but moving in that direction as the land headed downhill from where we had been.

We came, after walking for just over an hour, to a macadamed road. We followed this in a northerly direction until we encountered a telephone box. As a matter of course I lifted the receiver to find out whether it was working. In the past we had found that although the receivers had not been damaged in any way, the lines were dead.

On this occasion there was a short series of clicks, and then a woman's voice answered.

'Exchange. Which number do you require?'

I hesitated. I had not expected a reply and was thus unprepared.

'I'd like to make a call ... to Carlisle, please.'

'I'm sorry, caller. All trunk lines are engaged.'

There was a note of finality to her voice, as if she were about to close the connection.

'Er – could you get me a London number then, please?'

'I'm sorry, caller. All lines to London are engaged.'

'Would you ring me back when they are free?'

'This exchange is open for local calls only.' That final tone again.

I said quickly, 'Look, I wonder if you can help me. I'm

trying to get to the railway station. Could you direct me to it, please?'

'Where are you speaking from?'

I gave her the address of the telephone-box as printed on the plaque in front of me.

'Hold the line a moment.' She closed the connection and I waited. After about three minutes she came back on. 'The station nearest to you is in Warnham. Thank you, caller.'

The line cleared.

Sally was waiting for me outside the box and I told her what had been said. As I did so we both heard heavy lorries heading towards us and within a few moments seven troop carriers passed us. An officer was standing in the rear of one of them and he shouted something to us as they passed. We were not able to hear him. Something about the purposeful way they were heading somewhere was vaguely reassuring, even though it was the first time I had witnessed actual troop movements.

Silence fell as the trucks rumbled into the distance. Once again the countryside was still. We were the only people around.

I found Warnham on the map and we began our walk. Within a few minutes we saw more signs of military activity and civilian inactivity that alarmed us both.

Half an hour after we had left the telephone box we passed through a village. We walked the length of the street without meeting anyone, but in the windows of the last house we saw the shape of a man. I waved and called out to him, but either he did not see me or did not choose to, and he moved out of sight.

Outside the village we encountered an emplacement of heavy artillery manned by several hundred soldiers. There was a rough, but guarded, barbed-wire barrier between them and the road and as we approached it we were warned to move on. I tried to speak with the soldier but he immediately called an NCO. This man repeated the instruction, adding that unless we were out of the district by nightfall we would find our lives in danger. I asked him whether they were Nationalist troops and received no reply.

Sally said, 'Daddy, I don't like guns.'

We moved on towards Warnham. Several times jet aircraft flew overhead, low above the hedges. We could hear them all the time, the sound of their engines roaring above the countryside around us, but every now and again one would fly low above us. It terrified us every time, because of the speed, the suddenness, the explosive burst of noise. I discovered the remains of an old newspaper and tried to read it to learn what I could about what was going on.

It was a privately printed tabloid and one which I felt sure was illegal. We had heard on the radio two weeks before that the activities of the press had been suspended temporarily. The tabloid was virtually unintelligible; badly printed, abominably written, disgustingly slanted towards an overt racist xenophobia. It spoke of knives and leprosy, guns and venereal disease, rape, cannibalism and plague. It contained detailed instructions for the manufacture of such home-made weapons as petrol bombs, coshes and garrottes. There were items of 'news', such as mass rape by Afrim militants, and overwhelmingly successful raids by loyal military forces on Afrim strongholds. On the back page, at the bottom, I learned that the paper was published weekly for civilian consumption by the British Nationalist Army (Home Division).

I burned it.

The approach to Warnham Station was guarded by more

soldiers. As we came into their view Sally's hand took hold of mine and gripped it tightly.

I said to her, 'It's nothing to worry about, Sally. They're just here to make sure no one tries to prevent the trains running.'

She didn't reply, perhaps realizing that I was just as alarmed as she was at their presence. It meant, in effect, that the trains were still running, but that they were under military supervision. We walked up to the barricade and I spoke to a lieutenant. He was polite and helpful. I noticed that on his sleeve he had a strip of cloth on which was stitched: *Loyal Secessionists*. I did not refer to it.

'Is it possible to get a train to London from here?' I said.

'It's possible,' he said. 'But they don't run very often. You'll have to inquire, sir.'

'May we pass through?'

'Of course.'

He nodded to the two soldiers with him and they pulled back a section of their barricade. I gave the officer my thanks and we walked up to the booking office.

It was manned by a civilian wearing the normal uniform of British Rail.

'We want to go to London,' I said. 'Could you tell me when the next train's due?'

He leaned forward across the counter, put his face close up to the glass panel and looked through at us.

'You'll have to wait till tomorrow,' he said. 'There's only one way to get a train here and that's to ring through the day before.'

'Are you saying that no trains stop here?'

'That's right. Not unless someone wants 'em to. You have to ring through to the terminal.'

'But suppose it's urgent.'

'You have to ring through to the terminal.'

I said, 'Is it too late to get a train to stop here today?'

He nodded slowly. 'The last one went through an hour ago. But if you'd like to buy your tickets now, I'll ring through to the terminal for you.'

'Just a minute.'

I turned to Sally. 'Listen, love, we'll have to sleep tonight in the tent again. You don't mind, do you? You heard what the man said.'

'OK, Daddy. But can we definitely go home tomorrow?'

'Yes, of course.'

I said to the clerk, 'How much are the tickets?'

'Five pounds each, please.'

I pulled out of my pocket what remained of our money and counted it. We had less than two pounds.

'Can I pay for them tomorrow?' I asked the clerk.

He shook his head. 'Got to be paid in advance. If you haven't got enough now, though, I'll take a deposit and you can pay the rest tomorrow.'

'Will this be enough?'

'Should be.' He took all the notes and coins I had and dropped the money into a drawer, reckoned the amount on to a register and passed me a slip of printed paper. 'Bring this and the rest of the money tomorrow. The train'll be here about eleven in the morning.'

I glanced at the slip. It was just a receipt for the money, not a ticket. I thanked the man and we went back outside. It had started to drizzle. I wasn't sure how I was going to obtain the rest of the money by morning, but already a half-formed determination to steal it if necessary had come to mind.

At the barricade, the young lieutenant nodded to us.

'Tomorrow, eh?' he said. 'That's happened to a lot of people here. Have you come far?'

I told him we had.

'There are still many refugees around here,' he said, with some sympathy.

I was about to agree with him, when I realized that he was including us. I had not previously applied the word 'refugee' to our predicament.

'You should be all right in London,' he said. 'Our lot are getting things organized there.'

He gave me the name and address of a group in London who were able to find accommodation for the homeless. I wrote it down and thanked him. He expressed concern about what we were to do tonight.

'I could have offered to find you a billet,' he said. 'We've done it before. But there's something on. We might be moving out tonight. What will you do?'

'We have camping equipment,' I said.

'That's all right then. But if I were you, I'd get as far away from here as you can. We're being mobilized. The Nationalists are somewhere in the vicinity.'

Again I thanked him and we moved on. Both Sally and I had been comforted by his outgoing nature, by his apparent willingness to assist us. But what he had said had given us cause for alarm and I decided to heed his warning. We walked a long way to the south before trying to find somewhere to camp. In the end, we came across a suitable place on the side of a low hill, screened on three sides by woodland.

That night while we lay in the dark together we heard the sound of artillery, and more jet aircraft roared overhead. The night was lit by brilliant flashes from explosions to the north of us. We heard troops marching along the road on the other side of the hill, and a stray shell exploded in the woods behind us. That was a frightful moment. Sally clung to me and I tried to comfort her. The noise of the artillery itself remained constant, but the explosions from the shells varied between being quite close to us and some way away. We heard small-arms fire from time to time and the sounds of men's voices.

In the morning it drizzled again and the countryside was still. Reluctant to move, as if the act of doing so would restart the violence, Sally and I stayed in our bivouac until the last possible moment. Then at ten o'clock we packed our gear hastily and set off towards the station. We arrived at just before eleven. This time there were no soldiers. The station had been bombed and the railway track itself had been blown up in several places. We looked at the ruin in desolate horror. Later, I threw away the receipt.

That evening we were captured by a detachment of the Afrim forces and taken in for our first session of interrogation.

Isobel and I lay together in the dark. We were on the thickly carpeted floor of the living-room in her house. In the room above us her parents were asleep in bed. They did not know I was there. Though they liked me and encouraged Isobel to see more of me, they would not have been pleased if they were aware of what we had been trying to do in their sitting room.

It was after three in the morning and therefore essential we made no noise.

I had removed my jacket and shirt.

Isobel had taken off her dress, her slip and her brassiere. At this time we had recovered from the earlier embarrassing incident and had started seeing each other regularly again. Our physical relationship had developed to the point where she allowed me to remove most of her clothing while we kissed, and to fondle her breasts. She had never allowed me to touch her in the region of her pubes. In the past, most of the girls I had known had been free and adventurous about sex, and I was puzzled at Isobel's apparent lack of interest. Her reticence had been alluring at first but now I was beginning to see that she was genuinely frightened of sex. Although my interest in her had been initially almost entirely sexual, as we grew to know one another I had developed a deep liking for her and had made my sexual advances to her more and more gently. The combination of her physical beauty and her gaucherie was a continual delight to me.

After a prolonged session of kissing and petting I lay back on the floor and allowed Isobel to run her hand lightly over my chest and stomach. While she did this I found myself willing her to slide her hand into the top of my trousers and caress my penis.

Gradually her hand moved down until it was rubbing lightly against the cloth of the waistband. When her fingers did eventually explore the cloth, they came into contact with the end of my penis almost at once. Evidently unaware to that moment of my tumescence, she snatched her hand away at once and lay at my side, facing away from me, trembling.

'What's the matter?' I whispered to her after a minute or two, knowing both that I would get no reply and that I already knew what had happened. 'What's the matter?'

She said nothing. After a while I put my hand on her shoulder and found her skin to be cold.

'What's the matter?' I whispered again.

She still made no reply. In spite of what had happened I remained erect, unaffected by the trauma she experienced.

In a while she rolled back towards me and, lying on her back, took my hand and placed it on her breast. Like her shoulder, it was cold. The nipple was shrunken and lumpy.

She said, 'Go on. Do it.'

'Do what?'

'You know. What you want.'

I didn't move, but lay there with my hand on her breast, not wishing either to do as she said or to take my hand away altogether.

When I made no response, she took my hand again and thrust it down roughly to her crutch. With her other hand she dragged down her pants and laid my hand on her pubes. I felt warm, soft down. She started shaking.

I made love to her at once. It was painful for both of us and without pleasure. We made a lot of noise; so much so that I was scared her parents would hear us and come to investigate. As I climaxed, my penis slipped from its place and my semen went half into her, half on the floor.

I pulled back from her as soon as I could and lay away from her. Part of me remained detached, seeing wryly my experienced sexual artistry reduced to fumbling adolescence by the encounter with frigid innocence. But another, larger part of me lay curled up on the floor, unwilling to move.

In the end it was Isobel who moved first. She stood up and switched on the low-powered table-lamp. I looked up at her, seeing her slim young body completely naked for the first time, denuded for the first time of sexual mystery. She pulled on her clothes, kicked mine across to me. I put them on. Our eyes didn't meet.

On the carpet where we had been lying there was a small patch of damp. We tried to remove it with paper tissues, but a faint stain remained.

I was ready to leave. Isobel came to me, whispered in my ear that I was to push my motorcycle to the end of the road before starting it up. Then she kissed me. We agreed to see each other again the following weekend. As we crept out into the hall we were holding hands.

Her father was sitting on the bottom step of the stairs dressed in his pyjamas. He looked tired. As I walked past him he said nothing to me, but stood up and held Isobel tightly by her wrist. I left, starting the engine outside the house.

We had not used any form of contraceptive. Though Isobel did not become pregnant from that incident she did conceive a few weeks before we were married. From that time we had sex together only occasionally, and as far as I'm aware she only attained a full or pleasurable orgasm intermittently. Sex was never a joy for her. After Sally was born, what sexual dependence on one another that we had ever had grew less, and in due course I found myself turning to other women who were able to give me what Isobel could not.

In the good times, I would gaze at Isobel across a distance, remembering again the pale blue dress and her youthful beauty, the hopes and desires I once had, and a bitter regret would well inside me.

As the days passed since the abduction of the women by the Afrim soldiers, it seemed to me that while my own obsession with finding them grew stronger that of the other men diminished. I began questioning whether we were simply moving on day after day in the eternal search for a safe place to camp, and somewhere to obtain food, or whether we were pursuing our search for the women.

They were mentioned less and less often, and since the visit to Augustin's brothel it was sometimes as if they had never been with us. But on the day after we met the African guerrillas we were reminded forcibly of what might have happened to them.

We came to a group of houses that were marked on the

117

map as being a hamlet called Stowefield. At first sight it appeared to be no different from any of a hundred other small settlements we had come across in the past.

We approached it with our customary wariness, resolved that if the hamlet were barricaded we would retreat immediately.

It was soon clear that there had been barricades at one time. Where the windowless brick wall of one of the houses fronted the road, there was a pile of rubble which had been pushed aside to make a gap wide enough for a lorry to pass through.

With Rafiq, I inspected the ground beyond where the barricade had been and we discovered several dozen empty shotgun cartridges.

We went around the hamlet and looked in every house. Most of them had doors and windows open, so it was possible to go inside. Every single one was empty, and in many of them we saw signs that the evacuation had been hasty. We were fortunate in finding canned food in several of the houses and were therefore able to replenish our supplies.

We speculated about who might have raided the village. It was probably prejudice which prompted many of us to assume it was the Afrims, but we all knew of many incidents where they had done this kind of thing to small settlements they found barricaded.

There were no clues about what might have happened to the people who had lived here. There was damage and breakage inside every house, but that could have been caused by looters who came later. One house contained traces of an unfinished meal, but again it was not possible to draw a reliable conclusion from that. But towards the end of our search of the houses, one of the men discovered something and shouted for the rest of us to come.

I arrived with Rafiq. As soon as we saw what was there, he shouted at everyone, telling them to wait downstairs. He indicated that I was to stay with him.

There were the bodies of four young white women in the upstairs room. Each was naked and each appeared to have been sexually assaulted. My heart began to beat faster at the first sight of them, as I had been dwelling horribly on some of the possible fates that had befallen Sally and Isobel, but it took only two or three seconds to establish that these women were not them. The bodies were disfigured by death, but decomposition had not yet set in. There were signs of struggle, and there were dark stains of dried blood all over the floor. One of the women had a large wound in her chest, as if she had been stabbed. It was a horrible sight, and Rafiq and I backed away quickly. My heart continued to pound for a long time afterwards.

Rafiq and I discussed what we should do. I suggested that we bury them, but none of us relished the task of carrying the bodies downstairs. The alternative that Rafiq suggested was to set fire to the house. It stood apart from the ones nearest to it, and it was unlikely the blaze would spread to others.

We went and spoke with the others. Two of the men had been sick, the rest of us felt nauseated and despairing. Rafiq's suggestion was adopted, and a few minutes later, after a last check that there was nothing else to find inside, we fired the house.

We moved away to the other end of the village and set up a camp for the night.

I was one of the few men who worked in the cutting shop of the factory. In spite of the equal-opportunity legislation that had gone through Parliament in the last months of the government immediately prior to Tregarth taking office, there were still many different kinds of work which were exclusively or nearly exclusively the domain of women. In the wholesale cloth industry, cutting is one of them.

My only colleagues of my own sex were old Dave Harman, a pensioner who came in every morning to sweep the floor and make tea, and a youngster named Tony who tried to flirt with the younger women but who was treated by them all as a cheeky young urchin. He played up to that, maddeningly. I never found out his true age, but he must have been at least twenty, and I never understood what he gained from playing the adolescent game with the women. None of us mixed socially outside working hours, and I knew almost nothing about Tony, but because of the almost ceaseless round of teasing and sexual innuendo we had to put up with, there built up between us a kind of male bond against the vulgarity of the women.

My own relationship with the women was acceptable once we had overcome the initial problems.

For instance, it was thought by most of the women that I had been brought in by the management as some kind of supervisor or inspector, and whenever I attempted to speak to them I was treated with cold politeness. In this, my middle-class vowels did little to help. Once I had realized what the probable cause of the friction might be, I went to pains to let them know my position in the cutting shop. Of course, I did not mention who my father was. When all that was clear the atmosphere lightened, though there were still one or two women who maintained a slightly distant air. Within a couple of weeks things had relaxed to the point where I felt as if my presence was taken for granted.

With this relaxation came the growing vulgarity of behaviour. I had seen it from the first day with Tony, but the initial chill had protected me from it until a certain amount of familiarity set in.

In my relatively sheltered life to this point – sheltered in the sense that I had not mixed with large numbers of working people – I assumed that women were the more socially restrained sex. The changing national situation might have encouraged a general slackening of morality, because people were increasingly aware of the repressive new laws that Tregarth's government was introducing. There were strict controls on pub opening hours, smoking in public, use of cars, use of electricity and gas, talk of some basic foods being rationed, currency restrictions on overseas holidays, and new or higher taxes on all kinds of non-essential goods. Older people remembered the emergency powers that had been introduced during the Second World War, and grumbled that the current situation was more restrictive, without the excuse of a war going on. The reaction was a noticeable loosening of behaviour, almost as if in deliberate disobedience: public drunkenness and brawling every night of the week, a rash of cheaply made exploitation films suddenly appeared in cinemas and on TV, there was general rudeness in shops and other public places, and an alarming increase in street crime, notably against people from ethnic minorities. In my immediate experience, the women who worked with me in the cutting shop were a bawdy lot, foul-mouthed and aggressive. A typical working day was punctuated with obscenities, disgusting jokes and various direct and indirect references to either my or Tony's sexual organs. Tony told me once that shortly before I had come to the cutting-shop, one of the women, in a mock-serious kind of way, had unzipped the front of his trousers and tried to grab him. He told me this off-handedly, though I could tell he had been upset by the incident.

As the recession deepened we found out that the company was not receiving as many orders as it had in the past, and consequently we had less and less work to do. Tregarth's government had introduced new labour laws, which made it extremely difficult for companies to lay staff off. Redundancy was still in theory possible, but there was a high financial penalty to be paid, both to the member of staff but also as a taxation surcharge. From our point of view it meant our jobs were protected – none of the people I worked with had to leave.

Shortly after I joined the firm the length of our lunch break was increased from one to one and a half hours, and soon after that it was increased again, to two hours. Sick leave was encouraged by our employers, although after the government's temporary withdrawal of National Health benefits absenteeism was rare. At the time the first secessions from the armed forces were taking place, and most of the main sea ports were sealed off by government troops, our work dried up altogether.

Technically we were given two hours every day for lunch, but in reality we spent most of the time sitting around and trying to find something to do. For one week, Tony and I cleaned out the whole cutting shop, and repainted walls, but once that was finished there was no more work of that sort available. We joined the others.

Our group of workers soon seemed to me to have become a microcosm of our newly integrating society. Although more than half the women were from a white working-class background there were several Asians, two or three West Indians and a couple of young women who had come into the country on one of the African refugee boats. These two, who had come from Mauritania, had not been able to speak

English when they first arrived, but they were learning quickly.

Some of the women brought in packs of cards or board games from home. Magazines and paperbacks were read all the time, and passed around. At first I too used this extra time for reading, but there were disadvantages. The material the women liked to read was superficial trash about TV celebrities and pop stars, but when I brought in my own books I was mocked because of the supposed intellectualism. Anyway, if I read too long in the poorly lit room my eyes would begin to hurt. The cutting shop was wired for radio broadcasts, but by common consent none of us could stand the endlessly bland music or the official announcements. Television was not much better and in any event the portable black-and-white set one of the women brought in was immediately confiscated by our manager. Several women brought in such things as needlework or knitting, and others wrote letters in laborious handwriting. Few of us ventured out during the lunch-break. Once or twice, some of the women went out shopping together, but on the whole it was considered too dangerous in our part of London.

I don't know how it began, but several of the women were using the time to get together around a bench and play on an improvised Ouija board. None of them said anything about it to me. I only became aware of it when I took a stroll through the adjoining warehouse during one of these long breaks. The women were in a corner of the warehouse. Seven of them actually sat at the table and another ten or so stood around watching. The pointer they were using was an inverted plastic tumbler and the letters of the alphabet were scribbled on scraps of card around the edge.

One of the older women was asking questions into the air, while the tumbler spelled out the answers from under the fingertips of the seven participants. I watched fascinated for a while, unable to determine whether the women were actually moving the tumbler deliberately or not. Some of the 'answers' produced by the pointer made the women squeal with excitement and amazement. There was a lot of noise. Annoyed that I was unable to understand what was going on, I walked away.

At the far side of the warehouse, behind a stacked pile of rolls of cloth, I accidentally came across Tony and the younger of the two Mauritanian women. Although they were both fully dressed she was lying on her back with her legs apart, and Tony was on top of her. His hand was inside the front of her dress, holding one of her breasts. Neither of them saw me.

As I backed away there was the sound of several voices from the Ouija table. One of the women, in fact the other Mauritanian, broke away from the group and ran into the cutting room. Her friend must have heard this because she ran out from where she had been with Tony, and joined her. Soon they were speaking loudly and angrily, but one of them started crying. After that they stayed apart from the others, and by the end of the following week both of them had left the firm.

As night fell the house was still burning; the village was suffused with a dark orange glow, and the obstinately sweet smell of smoke.

The mood of the group had altered subtly. For me, as well as the other men, the assault on the four young women represented a physical proof of our worst fears about our own abducted women.

Individually, I think we were all horrified and numbed but collectively our reaction was one of more overt determination not to become involved in the civil war any more than we had to. The search for the abducted women was not mentioned. What I had seen in the house had only hardened my own resolution. It was Sally I was worried about, for she was just a child whose life had hardly begun. My daughter, not my wife, was uppermost in my concerns.

As darkness came on I moved away from the main group of men and went into a house not far from the one we had fired. Behind me there was the afterglow of the blaze. The flames had died now but the timbers would go on smouldering for hours. Smoke drifted past, reminding me of autumn.

I sat by myself in an old armchair in a downstairs room of the house I had gone into and brooded about what I would do in the morning.

Time passed. I became aware of the sound of engines but I ignored them. They grew louder, drowning my thoughts. I leaped out of my chair and ran through the house and into the small garden at the rear.

The sky was clear of clouds and a quarter-moon threw enough light to mark the ground. Because I had been sitting in the dark in the house my eyes adapted at once.

It took me only a couple of seconds to locate the source of the sound: it was a formation of helicopters travelling at a low height and speed from the south in a direction that would carry them over the village. As they approached I dropped to the ground, my hand tightening over the rifle. I counted the aircraft as they passed overhead: there were twelve of them. They slowed even more in the next few seconds, and landed in one of the fields beyond the village. The noise of the engines and vanes cascaded around me, a torrent of sound and battering down-draughts.

They had landed beyond a rise in the ground and from where I was lying I was not able to see them. I climbed to my

125

feet and peered over the hedge. I heard the engines ticking over together in a low, muted grumbling sound. None of them was showing any navigation lights.

I waited.

For another ten minutes I stood still, debating whether to rejoin the others. There was no way of telling why the helicopters were here, or whether they knew of our presence. Perhaps they had seen the smoke from the burning house, or the glow of the embers, but it was unlikely they would send twelve valuable helicopters to investigate.

With an abruptness that startled me, there was a burst of gunfire close by, and two or three loud explosions. I ducked down, my heart racing with fear. From the direction of the flashes I guessed that the guns were being fired from the far side of a large wood I had noticed earlier, running alongside the main road a short distance from the hamlet. There was further gunfire, more explosions. I saw a spout of white flame, then a red Very light shot up into the sky from the direction of the wood.

Almost immediately the helicopters took off, rapidly taking up their formation again. They swooped into the air and swung away towards the wood. Soon I could no longer see them, although from the racket of their engines I knew they were still near.

I heard a movement behind me: the house door opening, closing.

'Is that you, Whitman?'

I made out the dim shape of another man. As he came up to me I saw that it was Olderton, one of our group.

'Yes. What's going on?'

'No one knows. Rafiq sent me to find you. What the devil are you doing?'

I told him I had been looking for food and that I was going back to the main camp in a few minutes.

'You'd better come now,' Olderton said. 'Rafiq's talking of moving on. He thinks we're too close to the main road. Something's going on and he doesn't want to get caught up in it.'

'I think we ought to know what's happening before we move.'

'That's up to Rafiq, not you.'

'Is it?' For no reason I could determine I felt a taint of rebellion in being told what to do. In any event, I didn't want to discuss it with Olderton, a man I had often found obnoxiously stubborn and awkward. He always made me react against him in the same obdurate way, a habit I had not yet managed to break out of.

The sound of the helicopters in the distance took on a new note, and we went back to where I had been standing before, looking across the fields in the direction of the wood.

'Where are they?' Olderton said.

'I can't see.'

There was a renewed burst of gunfire, then a shrill, high-pitched whistling sound followed immediately by four explosions coming almost together. A brilliant ball of flame rose up inside the wood, then dwindled. I heard more gun-fire. One of the helicopters roared over the village. Another held a stationary position, a short distance away. From this machine came an explosive roar, and bright rocket trails scorched across at the trees. Olderton and I both reflexively ducked, but the missiles were not aimed at us. A second or so later there were four more loud explosions from within the wood. The whistling sound was repeated – it was a horrible and terrifying noise – and another four more explosions.

A new helicopter passed overhead, took up the stationary firing position.

'They're after something on the main road,' Olderton said.

'Who are they?'

'Rafiq thought they were Afrims. He said the helicopters looked as if they were Russian. I wouldn't know the difference.'

'So how did they form an air force?' I said.

Over at the main road the aerial assault went on. The helicopters were synchronized as if in a drill. As the explosion from one set of rockets died down, another gunship came in and followed up. Meanwhile, small-arms fire rattled from the ground.

'I think it might be those guerrillas,' I said suddenly. 'The ones we met yesterday. They've ambushed something on the main road.'

Olderton said nothing. As I thought about it the more likely it became. The men had obviously been concealing something, on that we had all agreed. If, as Rafiq had guessed, the helicopter gunships were supplied by Russia and manned by Afrims, then it meant the civil war had escalated to a new level of horror.

For a few more minutes the unequal battle went on. Olderton and I watched as well as we could, seeing only the flame of the explosions and the gunships as they came by overhead after their pass. I found myself counting the number of attacks made. After the twelfth aerial bombardment there was a brief pause. We could hear the helicopters regrouping in the distance. One of the machines suddenly came up from behind us. It flew over the wood again, this time without firing any of its rockets. It zoomed overhead then went to join the others. We waited again. From the direction of the wood there was now a steady glow of brilliant orange fire and from time to time the sound of small explosions. There did not appear to be any more gunfire.

'I think it's over,' I said.

Olderton said, 'There's still one of them around.'

To my ears it seemed as if the formation of gunships was moving away, but it was impossible for us to tell from our position crouched on the ground. I kept looking around but could not see any sign of the helicopters.

'There it is!' Olderton said. He pointed over to our right.

I could just make out its dark shape against the sky. It was moving slowly and near the ground. It showed no navigation lights. It came towards us steadily. Irrationally I felt it was looking for us. My heart began to beat rapidly.

The aircraft moved across the field in front of us, then turned. Climbing slightly, it flew directly over us. When it reached the smouldering remains of the house on the other side of the road it hovered.

Olderton and I went back into our house, climbed the stairs and watched the helicopter from an upstairs window. The machine was hovering immediately above the burnt-out ruin of the house and the draught from its vanes sent cinders scudding over the ground. The embers brightened fitfully, fiercely. Flames took hold again in some of the timbers, and smoke swirled up and across to us.

In the glow from the ground I could see the helicopter's cabin clearly. I lifted my rifle, took careful aim and fired.

Olderton leaped over to me and knocked the barrel aside.

'You stupid bastard!' he said. 'Now they'll know we're here.'

'I don't care,' I said.

I was watching the helicopter. For a moment I thought

129

my shot had had no effect. Then the engine of the machine accelerated abruptly and it lifted away. Its tail spun round, stopped, then spun again. The helicopter continued to climb, but it was moving to one side, away from us. The engine was screaming. I saw the helicopter check its sideways motion, but then it flipped again. It skidded down over the burnt-out house, disappeared from sight. Two seconds later there was a tremendous and long drawn-out crash. The ground shuddered and in the sudden glare of white and yellow fire we saw huge pieces of the aircraft hurled in the air, whirling erratically and dangerously.

'You cunt! You stupid bastard!' Olderton said again. 'Now the others will be back to find out what happened.'

I said nothing. We waited.

During the days after Isobel had left us, Sally and I were continually in a state of fear and disorientation. It was because this was at last the real crisis made real. It affected us, it was the breakdown of everything we had known before the start of the fighting.

Our marriage, jobs, possessions, home – all gone. I tried to protect Sally from seeing it like that, trying to pretend our troubles were only temporary, that a solution was in sight.

Isobel's absence produced some unexpected reactions. In the first place, I experienced quite distinct pangs of sexual jealousy. While we were married, living together, I knew that Isobel had both the opportunity and the motivation to take a lover, yet at no time did I suspect her of doing so. With all the present uncertainty, however, I found my thoughts turning to her often, wondering about her, what she was doing, if she might be with someone.

Secondly, I found I was missing her, however negative her attitude had often seemed to be.

130

We had never discussed it directly, but both Isobel and I had been aware of the future, of what would happen to us when Sally finally grew up and left home. We would probably have held on until then, but in reality that's when our marriage would have ended. It had of course never started. Alone with Sally in the countryside it felt as if the predictable course of our lives had ended abruptly, that from this point nothing more could be planned, that life had ended, that the future was the past.

An hour passed. After the crash of the helicopter, Rafiq and the others came over to find out what had been going on. We could not see the wreckage of the aircraft, as it had landed beyond the rise of ground in the field. After the first devastating explosion as it crashed, the helicopter had burned briefly, with several smaller explosions. Since then, there had been no sign of movement from the crash site and none of the other helicopters had returned. The night was quiet, with only the faint flicker of light from the wood to show that for a few minutes the war had been going on around us.

I found myself in an ambiguous position. Though I detected an aura of grudging respect over the shooting down of the helicopter, Rafiq and one or two others stated unequivocally that it had been a stupid thing to do. I knew they were right. We always feared reprisals for anything we did that one militia or another might think was out of line. Had the other gunships been aware of what I did it was certain that they would have attacked us. Somehow, we had escaped detection.

Now that the moment of action had passed, and the subsequent period of greatest danger, I was able to think a little more calmly about what I had done.

In the first place I was convinced that the pilots of the gunships were either Afrims or their sympathizers. And while it was generally conceded that, regardless of racial or nationalistic prejudices, the militant African refugees were the one common enemy, in my particular case the firing of the rifle had turned into my reaction to the abduction of the women. In this I still felt I differed from the other men, although as I possessed the only rifle in our group I was the only one in a position to make such a gesture.

Anyway, I had derived an unexpected but enthralling pleasure from the incident. I had hardly ever fired a rifle before, I certainly had never fired one intending to kill someone else, and the fact that I appeared to have either killed or seriously wounded whoever was in the helicopter signalled a fundamental change in my life. From here I had committed myself.

There was some discussion over what our next move should be. I was tired and wanted to get some sleep, but the others were debating whether to visit the wrecked helicopter or trek across to the wood and examine whatever it was that had been attacked by the Afrims.

I said, 'I'm against either. Let's get some sleep, then move away from here before dawn.'

'No, we can't risk sleeping here,' said Rafiq. 'It's too dangerous in these houses. We've got to move, but we need barter for food. We'll have to take what we can from the helicopter, then get as far away as possible.'

It was suggested by a man called Collins that there might be more of value in the wood. Several of the other men agreed with him. Anything that was considered a worthy target by the military forces was a potential source of exchangeable commodities. In the end it was agreed that we would break with our normal policy, and separate. Rafiq, myself and two others would approach the wrecked helicopter; Collins and Olderton would take the rest of the men over to the wood. Whichever group finished first was to join the other.

We returned to the camp at the other end of the village, packed our gear, and set off as planned.

The helicopter had crashed in the large field beyond the burnt-out house. It had been at least half an hour since there had been any sign of flames or explosions from the area of the wreckage, so we reckoned it would be safe to approach it. I was concerned about what might have happened to the crew. If they had been killed in the crash, from our point of view all would be well. On the other hand, if any of them were still alive we could be in an extremely dangerous position.

We said nothing as we moved towards it. When we reached the edge of the field we could see the shape of the wreck, like a huge smashed insect. There appeared to be no movement but we watched for several minutes in case.

Then Rafiq muttered, 'Come on,' and we crept forward. I had my rifle ready, but still doubted privately whether I would have the guts to fire it again. Rafiq's use of me as an armed assistant reminded me uncomfortably of the incident at the barricade.

The last short distance we moved on our stomachs, crawling forward slowly, prepared for anything. As we neared the wreck we realized that if anybody were still inside he would not be in any state to present a threat to us. The main structure had collapsed and one of the vanes had bitten into the cockpit.

We reached the wreck unchallenged and stood up.

We walked around it cautiously, trying to see if there was anything that we could liberate from the wreckage. It was difficult to tell in the dark.

I said to Rafiq, 'There's nothing here for us. If it were daylight—'

As soon as I spoke we heard a movement inside and we backed away at once, crouching warily in the grass. A man's voice came from inside, speaking breathlessly and haltingly.

'What's he saying?' one of the other men said.

We listened again, but could not understand. Then I realized it must be an African language, one I recognized only by the sound of it. Recent news broadcasts in the BBC had been doubled up with summaries in Swahili, which this man might or might not have been speaking.

None of us needed to speak the language to know instinctively what the man was saying. He was trapped and in pain.

Rafiq took out his torch and shone it on the wreckage, keeping the beam low in an attempt to prevent from seeing it anyone else who might be in the vicinity.

For a moment we were unable to make out coherent shapes, though on one patch of relatively undamaged metal we made out an instruction printed in the Cyrillic alphabet. We moved in closer and Rafiq shone the torch inside. After a moment we saw a man lying, trapped in the broken metal. His face, which was towards us, was wet with blood. He said something again and Rafiq shut off the beam.

'We'll have to leave it,' he said. 'We can't get inside.'

'But what about the man?' I said.

'I don't know. There's not much we can do.'

'Can't we try to get him out?'

Rafiq switched on his torch again and flashed it over the wreck. Where the man was lying was almost totally surrounded by large pieces of broken cockpit and fuselage. It would take heavy lifting gear to move.

'Not a hope,' said Rafiq.

'We can't just leave him.'

'We'll have to.' Rafiq returned the torch to his pocket. 'Come on, we can't stay here. We're too exposed.'

I said, 'Rafiq, we've got to do something for that man!'

He turned to me and came and stood very close.

'Listen, Whitman,' he said. 'You can see there's nothing we can do. If you don't like blood, you shouldn't have shot the fucking thing down. OK?'

To foreshorten the exchange, as I did not like the new tone in his voice, I said, 'OK.'

'You've got the rifle,' he went on. 'Use it, if that's what you want.'

He and the other two men started back across the field in the direction of the houses.

'I'll catch you up,' I said. 'I'm going to see what I can do.'

No one replied.

It took only a matter of seconds to establish that what Rafiq had said was true. There was no way of freeing the injured Afrim. Inside, his voice kept lifting and falling, interrupted by sudden intakes of breath. If I had a torch I would have been tempted to shine it inside and look again at him. Instead, I ran the barrel of the rifle into the space, and aimed it in the approximate direction the man's face had been.

But then I stopped.

I pulled the rifle out, stood up, and stepped back two paces. Then I lifted the barrel and fired two shots into the air.

The voice inside the wreckage fell silent.

Within two years of Sally's birth my relationship with Isobel had virtually disintegrated. We learned to suffer one another;

135

growing to dislike the sound of each other's voice, the sight of each other's face, the touch of our backs against each other as we lay in bed.

The man who came into the pub approached me directly. He told me his name was Joe and that he was my friend. At once I felt my guard go up, feeling that his approach was importunate. It was certainly uninvited and unwelcome. He had walked into the pub with several other men and women, none of whom I had seen before. They dispersed themselves about the crowded bar and started conversations with groups of the regulars. I tried to ignore Joe, but he was ready for that. I also tried to move away from him, but I was sitting at a table with my back to the pub wall and it was impossible to escape him without physically pushing past him. Anyway, I was on my own that evening and he was someone to talk to, or so I thought at first.

Joe asked me if I was happy with how things were going, if I felt nervous of the way some of the African refugees were forcibly ejecting people from their houses. I tried to be non-committal. The incidents I had seen on TV, and the many others I had heard about in conversations, had left me torn between a deep fear of it ever happening to me and my family, and an attempt to try to understand some of the wider implications.

Joe, my intrusive new friend, quickly explained that the purpose of the recently introduced laws was not to persecute the African immigrants but to protect them. He said that the new government took the view that they were essentially at our mercy, and that we should treat them as temporary dependants rather than as unwelcome intruders. The population of the country should not be panicked into unconsidered actions by the sight of one or two aliens who might be armed. As illegal immigrants they could only act outside the law for as long as it took the law to apprehend them. This was the whole purpose of the new Order Act.

I argued that I had heard many stories of persecution, of rape, murder and abduction. There was the notorious Gorton torture case, in which ten African women had been systematically degraded, raped, mutilated and finally murdered.

Joe agreed with me and said that this was precisely the kind of atrocity which the new Act was intended to prevent. By restricting the rights and movements of the aliens, they would be afforded a greater degree of official protection provided they themselves submitted to the various regulations. The fact that so far the majority of the Afrims had rejected this protection was only a further indication of their essential alienness.

He went on to remind me of John Tregarth's early political career, when, even as a Tory backbencher, he had made a name for himself by his commendable policies of patriotism, nationalism and racial purity. It was a measure of his sincerity that he had held to his views even during the temporary phase of neo-liberal xenophilia before the beginning of the emergency. Now he had risen to high office, the nation would see that its farsightedness in electing his party into government would be rewarded.

I felt increasingly nervous of Joe. He was dressed neatly in a dark business suit, and was wearing a clean white shirt with a tasteful dark-blue tie. These clothes did not fit with the rest of his appearance – he was heavily built, with a shock of unkempt hair, he had not shaved for two or three days and he smelt of stale sweat. He leaned closely towards me when he spoke and I could see that his front teeth were discoloured. A pale line, an old scar of some kind, ran back from his left eye towards his ear. The political arguments he was stating sounded increasingly like a prepared set of statements, which he had been made to learn and then rehearse.

I looked around the bar hoping for some way of getting away from him, but I was still hemmed in. He asked me what I thought of what he had told me.

I said neutrally that I was under the impression that Tregarth had come to power through the sponsorship of various business interests which had undertaken the expense of the campaign.

Again Joe agreed with me, pointing out that it is an expensive business to create an entirely new political party. The fact that they had been defeated at only one general election before taking office was further evidence of their immense popularity. He asked me how much I could contribute to party funds.

I avoided that by arguing that it was only through creating a rift in the existing Opposition that Tregarth had acquired any following at all, and that his party seemed to be maintaining strong support from some sectors of the business community.

We lapsed into silence for a while. I was wondering where this discussion was going to lead. I had always disliked Mr Tregarth and his extremist policies, but at the same time I did not like the way in which the present political situation was affecting my own life.

Joe would not leave me alone. He reminded me that Tregarth had come to power several months before the Afrim situation began, that he had not created the emergency but only responded to events as they developed. Finally, my friend asserted that there was no question of racial discrimination in the way the problem was now being handled. A difficult set of circumstances must be dealt with firmly, and for all the declared humanitarian motives expressed from some quarters, the fact remained that the Afrims were hostile and dangerous aliens and must be treated as such.

I finished my drink, but Joe did not offer to buy me another.

I caught up with Rafiq and the other two in the village and we moved on as a group in the direction of the wood. Rafiq said nothing about the man inside the helicopter. I had evidently overrated the importance of the incident.

As we came out of the village and joined the main road that ran through the wood, one of the older men who had gone with Collins came up to us excitedly.

'In the wood! Collins says it's there!'

'What is?' said Rafiq.

'He sent me to get you. We've found them.'

Rafiq pushed past him and walked quickly in the direction of the flames. As I followed, I glanced at my wristwatch, holding up the face to catch what little light I could from the moon. It was just possible to make out the time: it was half past three. I was feeling more weary with every minute and could not see us setting up another camp within the next hour. We knew it was hazardous to try to sleep during the day unless we were able to find somewhere well concealed.

As we came to the edge of the wood the air was thick with smoke. It was acrid and drifted low, making me feel threatened by its toxic quality. I had never smelled anything quite like it before, because it seemed to be a composite of many different kinds of fire. Overriding it all, though, was the stench of cordite; the flavour of war, the stink of a spent cartridge.

We approached the scene of the ambush. A heavy agricultural lorry had been parked broadside across the road. Not far from it was the wreck of the leading truck of the convoy. It had received at least one direct hit from the rockets of the gunships, and it was scarcely recognizable as having once been a vehicle. Behind it were the wrecks of several more: I counted only seven, although afterwards I heard Rafiq say that there had been twelve. How he worked that out, I do not know. At any rate, there were four trucks still burning. To each side of the road shrubbery had been ignited by the explosions and the smoke from this joined with that of the vehicles. There was not much wind and in the region of the trucks the air was virtually unbreathable.

I stood with Rafiq. We were trying to discern which side had been using the trucks. In this undeclared three-way civil war the opposing forces rarely displayed colours and it was unusual to see any kind of vehicle bearing identification marks. Logically, the trucks had been driven by Nationalist or Loyalist troops, as the helicopters had been shown to be piloted by the Afrims, but there was no way of telling. I thought the trucks looked as if they had been made in the USA, but none of us was sure.

A man came out of the smoke and stood before us. In the fitful light from the blaze we could see that it was Collins. He had tied a piece of cloth over his nose and mouth and now he was out of the smoke he was inhaling deeply.

'I think it was a Nationalist supplies convoy, Raf,' he shouted to us, then turned away to cough loudly and painfully.

'Is there anything for us?' Rafiq said.

'No food. Not much else.' He was still gasping. 'But come and see what we've found.'

Rafiq took a rag from his pocket and tied it around his face. I followed suit. When we were ready Collins led us past the remains of the first two trucks and up to the third. This one was not alight.

A rocket had landed directly in front of it, wrecking the driver's cab but not setting fire to the main part of it. The truck had then collided with the one in front of it, which had burned earlier but without affecting the other. The truck immediately behind it had been victim of a direct hit and its remains were smouldering. Eight or nine of our men stood around looking expectantly at Rafiq.

Collins gestured towards a crate lying on the ground. 'We found that on the truck.' Rafiq knelt before it, reached inside and pulled out a rifle. He laid it on the ground.

'Are there any more of these?'

'It's full of them.'

Just then, a truck at the far end of the line exploded, and we all reacted by crouching defensively. I was holding my own rifle and instinctively I backed away towards the nearest trees. I watched Rafiq.

He looked round. I heard him say, 'Is there ammunition?'

'Yes.'

'Get it off quickly. As much as we can carry. Kelk!' One of the men ran forward. 'Get a handcart. Empty everything off it. We'll carry the rifles on that.'

I stepped back into the trees, suddenly an observer.

It occurred to me that if the ammunition truck were to explode, then all of us around it would be killed or seriously injured. I noticed how much of the grass and shrubbery around the truck was blackened with heat, and how sparks from other trucks drifted nearby. I wondered if there was much diesel oil on the truck, or if there were any unexploded rocket shells in the vicinity. It was possible that rifles and the ammunition for them were not the only explosives on the truck and that some of it might explode simply by being manhandled. Though my fears were based on logical

141

grounds, there was an element of irrationality too ... a feeling, superstitious perhaps, that if I moved to assist the others I would somehow provoke disaster.

I stood amongst the trees, the rifle redundant in my hand.

Once, Rafiq left the others and stood with his back to the truck, staring towards me in the trees. He called my name.

I waited until the loading was finished to Rafiq's satisfaction. Then as four of them pushed the heavily loaded handcart away, I followed at a discreet distance until a campsite was selected at a good distance from the ambushed convoy.

I made an excuse to Rafiq that I thought I saw a figure lurking in the woods and had investigated. Rafiq was displeased and to appease him I offered to stand first guard on the liberated weapons. Another man, Pardoe, was told to share the watch with me, which lasted for two hours.

In the morning each man was issued with a rifle and ammunition. The rest of the night-time haul was stowed back on the handcart and covered with spare clothes, bags, water bottles, and so on.

In the weeks following, Sally and I were on our own. For some time we continued to live in our tent, but were fortunate finally in finding a farm where we were allowed to live in one of the labourers' cottages. The couple who lived in the farm itself were elderly and took little interest in us. We paid no rent, and we were given food in return for assisting with work around the property.

In this period we had a semblance of security, though we were never allowed to forget the growing military activity in the countryside.

The area was under the control of the Nationalist forces and the farm itself was considered to be strategic. Men from the army came in occasionally to help with the work, and an anti-aircraft battery was built in one of the outer fields, though it was never, to my knowledge, used.

At first, I had an overwhelming interest in the progress of the civil war but soon learned to curb this. I spoke only once with the farmer about the political situation and learned that he was either unwilling or unable to discuss it. He told me that he had once had a television and radio, but that they had been removed by the army. His telephone did not work. His only access to information about the outside world was through the army tabloid that was distributed free to all civilians. His occasional meetings with other farmers were uninformative, since they had all been placed in a similar position.

I spoke several times with the men from the army who worked on the farm. Here, too, I was not able to learn much. They had evidently been ordered not to speak with civilians about the progress of the war, and though this was not strictly adhered to it was plain that the major part of their knowledge consisted of the propaganda put out by their intelligence staff.

One night, in early October, the farm was the target of a raid by enemy forces. At the first pass of the reconnaissance plane, I took Sally to the best available cover, which with a bit of foresight I had selected soon after we arrived. It was a disused pigsty, which had the advantage of being constructed with stout brick walls. I had cleaned it out, and put a few rudimentary provisions inside: some candles, a couple of blankets, and so on. Sally and I lay inside until the attack was over.

Our cottage was not damaged, but the farmer's house had been destroyed. The couple were missing.

In the morning the commander of the Nationalist troops visited the farm and took away what remained of the equipment that had been dumped there. The anti-aircraft battery was abandoned.

For no better reason than an unwillingness to uproot ourselves, Sally and I remained in the cottage. Though we felt we were in a precarious situation, we didn't want to return to living under canvas again. Later in the same day the farm was occupied by a detachment of integrated Afrim and Secessionist soldiers, and we were questioned closely by the African officer in charge.

We observed the soldiers with great interest, as the sight of white men actually fighting alongside the Africans was new to us.

There were forty men in all. Of these, about fifteen were white. Both officers were Africans, but one of the NCOs was white. The discipline appeared to be good, and we were treated well. We were allowed to stay temporarily in the cottage.

During the next day the farm was visited by a high-ranking Secessionist officer. As soon as I saw him I recognized him from the photographs which had been published regularly in the Nationalist tabloid. His name was Lionel Coulsden, a retired senior army officer. Before the war he had become known as a prominent campaigner for civil rights. During the period of Afrim infiltration of private property in the towns and cities, he had renewed his commission in the army. When serious military hostilities broke out he had led the secession of many units of the army to the African cause. He was now a colonel in the rebel army, and was currently under sentence of death by the Tregarth régime.

He spoke personally to Sally and me and explained that we would have to leave. A Nationalist counterattack was

144

anticipated shortly and our lives would be in danger. He offered me an immediate commission into the Secessionist forces, but I turned it down, explaining that I had to consider Sally.

Before we left he handed me a sheet of paper which explained in simple language the long-term aims of the Secessionist cause.

These were a restoration of law and order; an immediate amnesty for all Nationalist participants; a return to the parliamentary monarchy that had existed before the civil war; the restitution of the judiciary; an emergency housing programme for displaced civilians; and full British citizenship for all contemporary African immigrants. It reflected exactly what I hoped would happen, but all our recent experiences had underlined the impossibility of a peaceful solution to the present chaotic fighting.

We were transported by lorry to a village about an hour away from the farm. This, we were told, was in liberated territory. We noticed that there was a small Afrim army camp situated nearby and we approached them for assistance in finding somewhere to stay temporarily. We were not greeted with the affability displayed by the Secessionist colonel, and were threatened with imprisonment. We left at once.

The village was a singularly unfriendly place and we suffered distrust and hostility from the few people we encountered. That night we slept under canvas in a field on the side of a hill to the west of the village. I heard Sally crying.

A week later we found a house standing in small grounds of its own. It was near a main road but screened from it by a wood. We approached it warily, but though we were met with some initial caution we were not turned away. The house was occupied by a young married couple who offered to allow us to shelter with them until we could find alternative accommodation. Their names were Ken and Rachel. We stayed for three weeks.

It was the first time I had seen Rafiq frightened, but it was also the first time I was truly frightened of him.

We were all tired after the events of the night and our nerves were stretched. Rafiq, in particular, betrayed the stress he was feeling. Unable to decide whether or not we should move on, he prowled to and fro clutching his new rifle, as if his authority would be undermined if he let go of it. The rest of us watched him uneasily, not liking this new insight into his character.

I was occupied with my own doubts. The consequences of our finding these weapons were alarming. Already I had overheard one remark about us forming an effective guerrilla organization against the Afrims. Some of the men wanted to go out and look for other, similar groups and band up with them. *Strength in numbers* and *they won't ignore us now* and *at last we can do something* ... all these were being said. I heard the phrase 'black bastards' used repeatedly, more often, in fact, than during those vengeful hours after the women had been abducted.

Rafiq was at the focus of my fears, as much as the mood of the other men was frightening me. Now, as never before, there was a sense that our actions would no longer be determined solely by him.

What made me so apprehensive about Rafiq was his apparent indecision. He muttered about the risks of staying put in the temporary encampment we had made just a short distance from the ambushed convoy. At the same time, if any of us talked about moving on, or looked as if we were packing our gear ready for a move, he shouted at us to stay still.

Both fears were understandable. We'd be discovered almost at once if anyone came to investigate what had happened. To move, though, laden down as we were with so many rifles, would be disastrous if we were seen by any of the participating militias. Rafiq had made himself leader of our group, so instinctively we were waiting for him to make a decision. But everyone, including Rafiq, knew that unless we did something soon, either the group would break up or we would replace him.

For the moment we stayed where we were, as by non-action we did at least seem to be making a decision.

With three of the other men I made an inventory of the rifles we now possessed. In addition to the ones carried by each of us, we had twelve crates. In each crate there were three rifles. There were also several boxes of ammunition. In all, the pile of weaponry was almost more than we could handle. We had loaded most of it on to our handcarts, but it was apparent that this could not be a permanent arrangement. Each one now required two men to pull it, and one more to push and guide from the rear.

I glanced at the other men sitting in a ragged group among the trees, their new-found rifles close at their sides. I looked beyond them to where Rafiq stood, lost in his own thoughts.

I felt that of all the men I had come nearest to Rafiq in recent weeks. In a while, I went over to him. He was not pleased to be interrupted, especially by me. I knew at once I had made a basic error of judgement in going up to him and realized I should have stayed with the other men.

He said, 'Where the hell were you last night?'

'I told you what happened. I thought I saw someone.'

'You should have told me. If it had been the Afrims they'd have shot you.'

I said, 'I thought we were in danger. I had my rifle and I was the only one able to defend us.'

I did not wish to tell him the truth.

'We've all got rifles now. You don't have to undertake hazardous missions for our benefit. We can look after ourselves, thanks very much, Whitman.'

The tone of his voice was not only bitter. It was impatient, irritated, distracted. His mind was on something else; my crossing to speak to him had only reminded him of the night before, it was not uppermost in his mind.

'You now have all the rifles you need,' I said. 'What are you going to do with them?'

'What would *you* like to do with them?'

'I think we should throw them away as soon as possible. They'll bring us more problems than they'll solve. Nothing but trouble. None of us is trained to use them.'

'You proved that last night,' Rafiq said. 'No, I'm not going to dump them. I have other ideas.'

I said, 'What are they?'

He shook his head slowly, grinning at me. 'You tell me something. What would you use them for, assuming you could get away with it?'

'I've already told you.'

'Wouldn't you barter them to other refugees? Or try to shoot down more helicopters?'

I saw what he was getting at. I said, 'It's not just the fact of having weapons. It's that if everyone has them, instead of one or two people, the effectiveness is lost.'

'So while you were number one with the rifle, it was all right. Now that distinction no longer exists, it isn't.'

I said, 'I gave you my arguments for having a rifle when

148

I first discovered it. One rifle represents a form of defence, but arming us all constitutes aggression. It forms us into a militia, and a lot of the men have personal scores to settle. You wouldn't be able to control them any more.'

Rafiq looked at me thoughtfully. 'Perhaps we agree more than I thought. But you still haven't told me what practical use you would put them to.'

I considered for a moment. I still had only one real motivation, however impracticable it might appear to be.

'I would try to do something about finding my daughter,' I said.

'I thought that's what you'd say. It wouldn't do any good, you know.'

'As far as I'm concerned, anything would be better than what we've done so far.'

'Don't you understand?' Rafiq said. 'There's nothing we can do about that. The best you can hope for is that they're in an internment camp, and that one day you might be able to find them. Seriously, I doubt it. Anyway, more likely they've been raped or murdered, probably both. You saw yesterday what they do to women.'

'And you can just accept that?' I said. 'It isn't the same for you, Rafiq. That was my wife and my daughter that they took. My daughter!'

'It didn't only happen to you. There were seventeen women taken.'

'But none of them were yours.'

Rafiq said, 'Why don't you just accept it, like the others have? There is nothing we can do to find them. We're outside the law. Approach any of the authorities and we'll be imprisoned immediately. We can't go to the Afrims because first of all we don't know where they are, and anyway we couldn't expect them to admit that they've abducted our women. We'll get no sympathy from the UN people. All we can do is continue to survive.'

I looked round angrily. 'You call this survival? We're living like animals.'

'You want to give yourself up?' Rafiq's tone had changed; he was trying to be persuasive now. 'Listen, do you know how many refugees there are like us?'

'No one knows.'

'That's because there are so many. Thousands of them, perhaps millions. We're operating in a tiny area of the country. All over England there are homeless people like ourselves. You said we shouldn't be aggressive. But why not? Every single one of those refugees has an excellent reason for wanting to participate. But circumstances are against him. He's weak. He has little food, no resources. He has no legal position. Err to one side and he is a potential danger to the military forces because he is mobile, because he sees the war being conducted – move too far in the other direction and he becomes politically involved. You know how the government treats refugees? As secessionist fraternizers. Do you want to see the inside of a concentration camp? So the refugee does just what we've been doing: he lives and sleeps rough, he congregates in small groups, he barters, steals and keeps out of the way of everyone else.'

'And has his women taken from him,' I said.

'If that's the way it has to be, yes. It's not an attractive state, but there's no ready alternative.'

I said nothing in answer to this, knowing he was probably right. I had long felt that had there been an alternative to the wretched vagrant life we had been leading we would have discovered it. But what we saw of the various organized bodies during the brief periods of interrogation made clear to us that there was no place any more for the displaced civilian. The major towns and cities were under martial law, smaller towns and villages were either under military control or had defended themselves with civilian militia. The countryside was ours.

After a minute or two I said, 'But it can't stay this way for ever. It's not a stable situation.'

Rafiq grinned. 'Not now it isn't.'

'Now?'

'We're armed. That's what the difference is. The refugees can unite, defend themselves. With rifles we can take back what is ours. We've found a way back to freedom!'

I said, 'That's insane. You've only got to leave this wood and the first detachment of regular troops will slay you.'

'A guerrilla army. Thousands of us, all over the country. We can occupy villages, ambush supplies convoys. But we'll have to be careful, have to stay hidden.'

'Then what would be the difference?'

'We'll be organized, armed, *participating*.'

'No,' I said. 'We mustn't become involved in the war. There's too much fighting already. What on Earth would you achieve? Just more people being killed.'

'We'll put it to the others,' he said. 'It'll be democratic, it can only work if we're all in favour.'

We walked back through the trees to where the others were waiting for us. I sat on the ground a little distance from Rafiq and looked at the handcarts laden with the armaments crates. I was only half listening to Rafiq. My mind was preoccupied with the image of a disorganized band of men, thousands of them in every rural area of the country, hungering for revenge against the impersonal military forces and civilian organizations on every side.

I saw that where once the refugees had represented a desperate but ineffectual neutral presence in the fighting, their organization into a fighting guerrilla force – if such a mammoth task could be accomplished – would only increase the chaos which was tearing at the country.

I stood up and backed away from the others. As I stumbled through the trees, with an ever-growing desperation to be away from them, I heard the men shout their approval in unison. I came to the edge of the wood, looked left and right, then straight ahead. I felt free for the first time in my life. Free, strong, safe.

I headed south.

I noticed the young woman sitting at a table a short distance from mine. Because she was half turned away, and had her head down while she was reading, I could not at first be certain it was her. As soon as I was, I stood up and walked over to her.

'It is you, Laura?' I said.

She stared at me in surprise, but recognized me at once.

'Alan! '

It was not like me to dwell on past affairs but I had been walking through Hyde Park when I remembered Laura. I knew she liked to go to the restaurant in the centre of the park at lunch, because I had been there with her several times in the past. Remembering her made me think about her and I wondered why we had drifted apart. We'd had a pretty good thing going. As I walked towards the restaurant I was even wondering if I would see her there, but when I arrived there was no sign of her. I sat down at a table near one of the picture windows, and ordered a salad. I stopped thinking about her. But then she must have come into the restaurant after me, because although I had been thinking about her, it had never occurred to me that I might really see her.

We laughed and talked while I stood by her table, catching

up briefly, like two old friends. She was looking different from the days when I knew her: her hair was shorter, she was wearing spectacles I had not seen her in before.

After a few minutes she moved to my table.

'Why are you here?'

'Isn't that obvious?'

'You came for lunch.'

'Yes. That too.'

We stared at each other across the table. 'Yes.'

We ordered some wine to celebrate with, but it was over-sweet. Neither of us wanted to drink it, but we could not be bothered to complain. We toasted each other and the rest didn't matter. While we ate I was trying to work out why I had come here. I was pleased to see her, and she seemed pleased to see me. Had we both gravitated here in the hope of a reunion? It could not have been only a seeking for the past. What had I been thinking during the morning? I tried to remember, but memory was inconveniently blank.

'How is your wife?'

The question that had been so far unspoken. I had not expected her to ask it.

'Isobel? The same.'

'And you are still the same.'

'No one changes much in two years.'

'I don't know.'

'What about you? Are you still sharing that flat?'

'No. I had to move. It became impossible with one of the guys. He was doing drugs, and there were a couple of police raids. I decided to get out. I looked around and managed to find somewhere to buy. Now I'm in debt, but at least I'm secure.'

'Semi-secure,' I said, thinking about the way houses were

153

being taken over in some of the northern towns. That had only just started then.

'London's a big place. No one's going to find my tiny flat, let alone throw me out of it.'

'Of course. The same with us.'

'Your cosy house in the suburbs.'

'Laura, I only live there because it's close to the college.'

'You don't have to stay. You used to say you wouldn't.'

'Well. I'm still there.'

We finished our meal, drank coffee. Silences began to appear in our conversation. They were awkward. I began to regret meeting her. But she was still beautiful, and I had forgotten that sharp and knowing look she had, which had always acted as a lure for me and a buffer against me. I had never been able to resist her although she sometimes drove me to despair. I couldn't get enough of her. Of all the women with whom I had had relationships, Laura Mackin was the one I could never forget.

'Why don't you leave her?'

'You know why not. Because of Sally.'

'That's what you said before. Every time.'

'Every time it was true. It still is.'

Another silence.

'You haven't changed, have you? I know damn well that Sally's just an excuse. This is what went wrong before. You're too weak to disentangle yourself from her.'

'You don't understand.'

But she did. She said now, 'Alan, you always hurt me, you know. But I still want you.'

'Even now?'

'Even now.'

We ordered another pot of coffee. I wanted to end the conversation, leave her here. Instead, it was easier to carry on. I had to acknowledge that what she said about me was true. And always that thought in the back of my mind: one more time with Laura would be amazing. I started thinking about her body, remembering some of our times together.

She noticed. 'Forget it, Alan.'

'You always could read me.'

'Yes, and I still can't say anything that will change you.'

'No.'

'I've tried too often in the past. You realize that this is why I wouldn't see you any more?'

'Yes.'

'And nothing's changed.'

I said, as plainly as I could, although an hour earlier nothing could have been further from my mind, 'I am in love with you still, Laura.'

'I know. That is what is so difficult. And I love you for your weakness.'

'I don't like you saying that.'

'It doesn't matter. I only mean it.'

She was hurting me in the way she had done before. I had forgotten this about Laura: her capacity to give pain. Yet I did the same to her. I knew what I did to her, and she knew the effect she had on me. But in a sense it was what thrilled us about each other – the constant risk, the not knowing. And what I had said to her was true, even thought it had arisen spontaneously during this unplanned meeting. In spite of everything I continued to love her even though I had not been able to admit this to myself until I ran into her here. Of the women I had known outside my marriage, Laura was the only one for whom I had deeper feelings than those of physical desire. And the reason for this was because she saw me and understood me for what I was. Though it pained me, Laura's appraisal of my inability to confront my relationship

155

with Isobel was for me an attractive quality. I don't know why she was in love with me, although she had always said she was. I had never been able to come to understand her fully. She existed in a kind of personal vacuum, living in but not belonging to our society. She had no immediate family. Her mother was an Irish immigrant living in Liverpool, and had died giving birth to Laura. Her father was a West Indian seaman. She had never met him, and did not even know if he was still alive. Her skin was a lovely golden brown, her features full-fleshed and earthy. Her beauty and elemental qualities had always driven me to the heights of passion and desire, but of course in the end I turned out to be a disappointment to her. She was to become one of the first victims of the Afrim situation, killed during a police baton charge in the second London demonstration. That day in the park restaurant was the last time I ever saw her.

I recognized the leader of the group as the man I had met in the ruined village when I was searching for food. He had been plundering the remains of a helicopter that had crashed some time earlier. He had told me his name was Rafiq, but it had given me no clue as to his origin. The group he was leading consisted of about forty individuals, including several children. They were not well organized.

I watched them from the upper floor of the empty house, hoping they would not make so much noise that Sally would wake up. We had had a long and distressing day and were both hungry. The group was obviously looking for somewhere they could camp, and although one or two of them glanced over at where I was hiding it apparently didn't meet their needs. The house was a temporary refuge only for Sally and me. As winter approached I knew we ought to find more permanent quarters and I had been thinking about quitting the countryside and trying to find accommodation in one of the towns. I was nervous of that, because I already knew that trying to get in past the barricades was almost impossible. The only hope would be to come towards the town from across fields and hope to find a garden or a back alley that was not secured.

I was still thinking about this as two of the men kicked down the door of the house opposite and went inside to search. The immediate problem I faced was whether or not we should make our presence known to these arrivals. Sally and I had survived quite well on our own. We had only moved from the house owned by Ken and Rachel when they told us, clearly frightened, that unregistered civilians, and those sheltering them, would be sent to internment camps if captured. They showed us a handbill that had been pushed under the door of their house. After three weeks with them we had started to settle down to a daily routine, and I had felt Ken appreciated the help I had given him in keeping the house provisioned. Rachel had liked Sally. Gradually we formed a cohesive little group, our initial worries about each other long gone. Although the ruling about not sheltering unregistered people was withdrawn soon after it was announced, reluctantly we all judged it best that we should move on. For two days after we left Sally and I wandered through the countryside, sleeping in our one remaining tent. We were both glad to find this unoccupied house, where there were beds we could use.

I watched the new group indecisively.

If we continued to operate on our own there would be less danger of being captured, but to join a larger group would almost certainly mean that food supplies would be more regular and other people would help make decisions about where to stay, and so on. A glimmer of civilization. On the other hand, we would lose some freedom of movement.

Neither staying alone nor joining up appealed, but in the time we had been with Ken and Rachel we had listened to the news bulletins from continental radio stations and learned with horror the true extent of the civil war in Britain. Within a few days of the first shootings it had degenerated into a chaotic and dangerous state of warring groups, large and small, different forces claiming authority or administration, and desperate shifts in allegiance. Different militias had sprung up in many different parts of the country. Meanwhile, African refugees continued to arrive, and without the infrastructure of conventional aid organizations these people were soon drawn into organized resistance groups. Sally and I had already experienced much of the resulting confusion, and it continued yet, but through following the radio news in the last three weeks I had at least been able to glimpse the larger picture. I realized that there were thousands of people like us, perhaps hundreds of thousands, ordinary members of the public, who had been displaced from their homes and jobs and were having to eke out a precarious existence as best they could. We were, in my view, the main casualties of this war I had known little about.

Most of the refugees were thought to be in the Midlands and the north, and up there conditions were supposed to be worse. There were fewer of us in the south, and it was thought to be easier. I wondered what these people who were speculating really knew.

In a while the group of refugees below me started to organize themselves better, and I saw two or three tents being pitched. A man came into the ground floor of the house and filled two buckets with water. A fire was lit in the garden and food was laid out.

Then at last I noticed one of the women who was looking

158

after two young boys. I had seen her twice already without recognizing her. She was trying to get the boys to wash themselves, though without much success. She looked dirty and tired, her hair tied untidily into a rough bun behind her head. It was Isobel.

If anything this should have made my indecision greater, but instead I went downstairs and asked Rafiq if Sally and I could join his group.

I was heading south. Alone, I felt more secure than I had done with Rafiq and the others because I was now entirely responsible for every decision. I had left my rifle with Rafiq's group, and had no other weapon. I carried only my bag containing a few personal possessions, a sleeping-bag and some food. I was able to avoid unwanted encounters with military forces, and found that my treatment at barricaded villages or defended houses was easier than if I had been with a group. The weather stayed dry and warm, so on the first night I slept under a hedge, the second in a barn. On the third night I was given a room in a house.

I came into contact with another group of refugees during the fourth day. Once initial caution about each other had been overcome, I spoke for some time with their leader, a man who told me to call him Smith. I don't suppose that was his real name – he called me by the name I gave him: Terry. We were both hiding something.

Smith asked me why I had left Rafiq and the others. I told him about the rifles and what Rafiq intended to do with them. The man and I agreed on the terrible potential consequences. I also told him about my search for my wife and daughter.

We were speaking to each other in what had once been a car park of a pub. The rest of his group were preparing a meal and taking it in turns to wash in the kitchen of the abandoned building.

'Was your group as large as ours?'

'Originally it was larger,' I said. 'Before the raid there were thirty-nine men and seventeen women.'

'Were the women in your families?'

'Mostly. There were three single women.'

'There are forty-five of us. And we have more women than men.'

Smith told me about a recent incident when they had been rounded up by some Nationalist forces. The younger men had been given two choices: they could be interned in concentration camps, or they could sign up to join the army. This matter still had not been resolved when by good fortune a United Nations inspection team had arrived at the camp. Most of the young men rejoined the group, but a few stayed behind to fight with the Nationalists.

I made a remark to the effect that one side appeared to want the men, while the other wanted the women.

Smith said, 'Are you sure it was Africans who took your women?'

'Yes.'

'Then I think I know where they might be.' He glanced at me, as if to judge what my reaction might be. 'It is only a rumour.'

'I've learned that rumours are the only reliable source.'

'Then you should know that the Afrim command has set up several brothels of white women for its troops.'

I stared at him, shocked and silenced as his remark sunk in. After a moment I said, 'Sally is just a child.'

'My wife is here in this group,' he said. 'It's something we have to be guarded against. All we can do is hide until the war is over.'

I was given a meal and we exchanged as much information about troop movements as we knew. They wanted to know details about Rafiq's group, and I gave them directions to where I had last seen them. Smith said that maybe combining the two groups into one larger one would mean they could defend themselves better. The longer we spoke, though, the more he kept returning to the subject of the cache of rifles. I wished I had not mentioned them.

I asked him for more information about the rumoured brothels. A sudden dread certainty was in me, that this was the fate that had befallen Sally and Isobel. It disgusted and frightened me, and I could barely think about the possibility without a gut-wrenching sense of revulsion. The only glimmer of hope, if what he said was true, was that it meant they were still alive. And if I could find out for sure where they were, I could try approaching one of the humanitarian relief organizations, and plead with them for their help.

Smith said, 'I've told you everything I know.'

'But you haven't said where.'

'I wasn't told.'

'You must have some idea!'

'It was just a rumour. Somewhere to the east of Bognor, they thought.'

'One of the seaside towns?'

'Maybe.'

I tried to remember which towns were in which position along the coast on the eastern side of Bognor. Brighton? Or was it Worthing? I had been to Worthing. This was the place where I had discovered the bungalow with the hidden petrol bombs.

For a few minutes, Smith and I scanned the maps we had of that part of the coast. Worthing did seem the most likely of the towns. It was about a day's walk to the south-west of where we were at the moment. Rafiq's last known position was a similar distance to the north.

I thanked Smith and other members of his group for the food and information, and left them. They were breaking camp and preparing to move on. Another place they had heard of, another rumour, where there was a large house they could get into. They would be safe there for a few days.

It was getting dark, so I camped for the night in a church-yard, surrounded by scores of broken tombstones. No one recently seemed to have any claim on the dead, so I assumed the vandalism was from the past.

The part of the coast to which I was heading was one I knew slightly. There is a string of seaside towns crammed into the flat land between the sea and the South Downs, with Bognor Regis at the western end, and Brighton to the east. These places, with names like Littlehampton and Lancing, all run into one another, combining to make a long strip of suburban-style resorts very much like one another. In recent times they had become towns where many people liked to go to when they retired, but when I was a child most of them were the sort of places where families took seaside holidays. My parents had taken me and my two brothers to Worthing for one such holiday, but I was so small at the time that I can barely remember it.

After a morning's brisk walk across the windy Downs, I came down from the hills and began to see the edges of urban development. I crossed several roads and saw more and more houses. Most of them appeared to be deserted, but I was so used to seeing abandoned houses, and so familiar with the unpredictable threats they sometimes contained, that I did not investigate further.

From the sign over the shuttered window of a former Post Office I discovered I was on the outskirts of Worthing itself.

I could already glimpse the sun reflecting off the calm sea ahead of me when I came across a well made barricade built across the road. There appeared to be no one manning it. I walked up to it as openly as possible, prepared always to take evasive action should there be any trouble.

The shot, when it came, took me by surprise. Either they were using blanks, or the shot was intended to miss, but the bullet or pellets came nowhere near me.

I crouched and moved quickly to the side. A second shot came, this time missing me narrowly. I heard a bullet ricocheting off the road surface. I dived gracelessly to the ground, falling awkwardly on to my ankle. I felt it twist under me and an agonizing pain ran through my leg. I lay still.

My new friend went over to the bar, spoke to one of the people with whom he had come into the pub, then ordered something. When he returned to my table he brought back only one glass of beer, for himself. He sat down, and looked at me over the froth as he took a long first sip. He asked me if I had had enough time to make up my mind.

'About what?' I said.

'If you are going to make a contribution to our funds.'

Annoyed with him I left the table, pushed past him and went to the bar to get myself a drink. I noticed that he also walked away from the table, which I was glad to see. However, after the barman had passed me a beer, I turned and found my new friend standing next to me.

'We know where you live, Whitman. We know where your child Sally goes to school.'

'Just leave me alone,' I said, my heart suddenly racing with fear.

The man raised a hand as if to try to reassure me and began telling me a joke. It was the first in what turned out to be a series of stories, all with flagrantly racist subjects. He laughed at each one himself, with his eyes closed and his mouth wide open.

I noticed that at some of the other groups of drinkers, where this intrusive man's associates had dispersed themselves, were starting to laugh out loud. At one table in the corner near the door, there was much shouting and hilarity, with some of the pub regulars joining in and telling their own jokes.

I kept backing away from the man, but he insisted on staying close to me.

Finally, he said, 'So you're an Afrim lover, right? A bleeding liberal?'

'Go away.'

'You're on your own, mate. No one else wants them in the country.'

'I don't care.'

'How long before they kick you out of your house? Don't say it'll never happen. Half the white population of Leicester has been displaced. You been down to Ealing lately? Want to catch TB from one of them? Ealing's the place for that. Or you want to see Sally beaten up and robbed?'

By this time I was terrified of the man and anxious to move away from him. But I did not want to leave just because of him. I had come to the pub on purpose. Late every evening there was a striptease show and I always liked to stay for that. I could see a couple of the pub staff getting the platform ready at the far end of the bar.

I rallied against the man. 'I'm not giving you money, so just fuck off and leave me alone!'

'So what's scaring you, Whitman?'

'I said fuck off, you racist bastard.'

'OK, mate. You're asking for it.'

The main lights in the bar were dimmed and two spot-lights shafted down at the platform. The first of the strippers pushed her way through the crowd and leapt bravely on to the tiny space. Loud recorded music blasted into the room and she began gyrating her supple hips. She was a young black woman, with a tall, voluptuous body, already scantily dressed in a tiny costume glistening with sequins. Many of the men in the bar began whistling and cheering. If I had not been pressed up against the doorway with this man looming over me, I would have been one of them, crowding as close to the platform as possible.

The man gave me a sinister sideways look, then raised his glass and swiftly drank the rest of his beer. He burped with a hand over his mouth and turned to put down the glass on the nearest table. I grabbed the opportunity and slid quickly through the door and out into the chill night. As I strode through the car park towards the main road, I saw the door open and close behind me, and I knew the man was follow-ing me. I heard quick footsteps.

I was terrified of what he would do to me if he caught up with me outside in the dark, so I simply abandoned all pretence of being unconcerned and broke into a sprint. I ran down the side of the main road, with the traffic going past in a blaze of headlights. At the first intersection I briefly paused and looked back: he was running after me, but I was younger and slimmer than him and had already gained a distance away from him.

I dashed off down the road to the right, away from the direction of my home, then almost immediately saw a small close of detached houses. I hurried along the hedged pathway, getting out of sight before the man had reached the main intersection. Taking no chances, I leapt over a low garden wall, landed on someone's lawn, then threw myself to the ground behind some shrubbery. I lay still, trying to quieten my frantic breathing.

If the man was still trying to follow me I had managed to escape him, because I squatted there for ten minutes with no sign of him. I eventually emerged, still frightened, but he was nowhere in sight. I walked cautiously back to the intersection, staying close to the wall, ready for instant flight should he appear.

At the road crossing, everything seemed reassuringly normal, the cars and buses accelerating away whenever the lights changed. There were some take-out food shops by the corner, and several people were in these, waiting while food was prepared.

I glanced down the road in the direction of the pub, but no one seemed to be standing around.

I walked past the shops, then along the main road, heading back towards where I lived. It was almost possible to push the incident aside, but the man had succeeded in making me think about some of the changes that were taking place in our neighbourhood.

I noticed, for instance, that two of the side roads had newly extended kerbs at the point where they met the main road, intended to slow down any traffic as it turned in. One of the streets even had a gate by the entrance, wide enough to seal off the road, although it was open as I walked past.

When I paused at one street to look along it, two men suddenly appeared from the garden close to the corner. They said nothing to me, but one of them was carrying a powerful torch, which he shone against me. I raised a hand and backed off. The torch went out at once.

Early on in the incident in the pub, before I felt threatened by him, the man was talking about the local Afrim settlement, which had been set up by the council in the park next to the town hall. It was supposed to be a temporary holding camp, a secure one, guarded during daytime and locked at night. Secure or not, there were many stories locally saying that the area had become a no-go zone after dark. I knew this was almost certainly true and I had deliberately taken a route to the pub, and now home from it, that was several blocks away from the camp.

I hated the thoughts all this gave rise to. I wanted to believe that life was going to carry on as before, that the arrival of so many refugees in the country would not drastically change anything, that the people like the racist in the pub were just an extremist minority. I knew, though, that I was closing my eyes to a real and changing situation.

When my walk home took me closest to the town hall area I saw groups of men and youths standing about in the streets. Many of them were drunk, and there were piles of bottles and fast-food containers discarded in the street. The men looked at me expectantly as I walked by, but I made no eye contact and passed them as soon as I could. I felt they were waiting for some excuse to provoke an incident, if not with the refugees themselves then with anyone they might think were sympathizers.

I reached the side road where we lived without any further incident. I walked quickly, glad to be almost home. But halfway along, in the driveway of one of the larger houses on the side opposite to ours, there was a police van. It was parked without lights, but its engine was running quietly and there was an internal light. There were six men inside, wearing protective gear: helmets with metal face-masks raised, strengthened jackets, gauntlets.

I knew at last that events were already picking up a destructive momentum, and that a humane resolution to the refugee problem was no longer possible.

Sally was overjoyed to be reunited with her mother, but Isobel and I greeted each other in a guarded way. Once again we were a small but cohesive family, though, and there was happiness in that thought. For a while I was reminded of a period in the early years of our marriage, when it had seemed that the presence of the child would make up for everything else that was wrong between us. I talked with Isobel about practical things, telling her of our attempts to return to London, and what had happened since. She told me how she had met and joined Rafiq and his group, and we remarked again and again on the sheer good chance that had brought us together again.

We slept together that night, the three of us, and although I felt Isobel and I should try to re-start our sexual relationship, I was incapable of making the initial move. Isobel was silently awake in the dark beside me, and although we lay in each other's arms we did not make love. Sally was deep asleep, near to us but not in the same tent. At the time I pretended to myself that it was Sally's close presence that put me off, but afterwards I realized that she was probably just an excuse.

Fortunately for us, and for all the refugees like us, the winter of that year was a mild one. There was a great deal of rain and wind, making the fields and lanes muddy, but only a short period of severe frosting. We established a semi-permanent camp in an old church. We were visited several times by Red Cross workers, and both military sides knew of our presence. We were usually warm and dry, and there was enough food to go round. The winter passed uneventfully, the only real handicap being the continuing absence of news of the progress of the civil disorder.

This quiet period was when I first saw Rafiq as some kind

of social visionary. He would talk thoughtfully of enlarging our group and establishing a recognizable unit which would be self-sufficient until the troubles had been resolved. He was an intelligent man, who said he had received a university education, although he did not say where. By this time, all of us had abandoned any hope of ever returning to our homes, and we realized that we would be ultimately in the hands of whichever side succeeded in creating a working government. Until then, Rafiq convinced us we should sit tight and await developments.

I think I grew complacent in this period. I was directly under Rafiq's influence and spent many hours in conversation with him. Though I grew to respect him and considered him my equal in many ways, I think he despised me, perhaps because I was incapable of committing myself to a firm political viewpoint. He told me he had been an industrial activist before losing his home, and he frequently used left-wing jargon, but I never did find out much about his background. He often seemed confused to me, sometimes bitterly complaining about the way he had been treated by the new arrivals, when he felt that he and others had been working to help them. At other times, he would fulminate about the intolerant and deeply conservative Reform government, and the racist impact of their policies.

Several other groups of refugees came to the church during the winter, staying for varying periods of time before moving on. We came to see our establishment there as a kind of nucleus of the homeless situation. In our own way we were prospering. Our semi-permanent status lent us a kind of stability and people who came to us often mentioned that they had heard about the work we were doing. The only work we were doing was in truth the work of survival, but none of us said anything.

With the coming of the spring, we soon saw that we were not the only faction which had used the lull in the hostilities to consolidate a position. In the late March and April we frequently saw military aircraft in the sky. One or two of our group said they could recognize makes of aircraft and they said many of them were foreign in origin. Troop activity renewed, and we were often woken by long columns of lorries passing on the road outside the building. Once we heard heavy artillery in the distance.

We had acquired a radio and it had been made to work. To our frustration, however, we were unable to learn much of use from it.

The operations of the BBC had been suspended, and replaced with a one-channel station called 'National Voice'. The content of this was similar to the tabloids I had seen: political rhetoric and social propaganda, interspersed with hours of continuous music. All continental and foreign stations were now being jammed.

We learned at the end of April that a major Nationalist offensive had been launched against rebel and alien groups in the south. The forces loyal to the crown were reported to be sweeping through the area in which we were established. Although we maintained a constant vigilance, we saw nothing. Every week or so another convoy of military trucks would roar slowly down the road, but there was no fighting that we could detect. However, these reports did make us concerned, because if there was any truth in them it could lead to more activity around us.

One day we were visited by a large delegation of United Nations welfare organizers and humanitarian aid observers. They showed us government directives which listed the groups of participants in the hostilities which were to be treated as dissident factions. White civilian refugees were included as dissidents.

The UN people explained that these directives had been issued some weeks before. But, as had happened several times, they had been withdrawn soon after. This continued the familiar uncertainty of our status. They advised us either to surrender ourselves to UN rehabilitation centres or to move on. They were giving us this advice, they said, because large numbers of Nationalist troops were in the area and apparently getting ready for another offensive.

That night we debated all this at length. In the end, Rafiq's wish that we should continue to live outside the law was carried. He argued, and we eventually accepted, that while many groups of refugees remained at large we represented a substantial but passive pressure group. They couldn't ignore us for ever. In the end they would have to resolve the conflict and rehouse us. To surrender to UN rehabilitation would be in effect to nullify this small level of influence. Anyway, from everything we had heard from people we met the conditions in overcrowded and understaffed camps were by all accounts worse than ours.

Several of the people in Rafiq's group did, though, go to the camps. In most cases they were the people with children. Most of us stayed with Rafiq and in due course we moved on from the church.

Before doing so, we had agreed on our daily tactics. We would move in a broad circle, returning to the vicinity of the church every six weeks. We would go only to those places which, either from our own experience or from what we had heard from other refugees, we knew were relatively safe for overnight encampment. We were equipped with as much camping equipment as we would need, and had several handcarts. We had a well established system of foraging and barter.

For four and a half weeks, we travelled as planned. Then we came to an area of flat farmland which was reported to be under Afrim control. This had no effect on our policy, as we had often passed through Afrim territory before.

We were not molested in any way on the first night.

I spent the afternoon at the college in a mood of withdrawn depression. I conducted three tutorials, but I was unable to concentrate fully. Isobel was uppermost in my mind. I was feeling guilty.

I had recently concluded an affair, in fact only two weeks before. It had been reasonably clean-cut at the end: the woman and I drifted apart by mutual consent, and there were relatively few emotional upheavals to contend with. The whole thing had been a reaction for me against Isobel's attitude to sex, or at least her attitude to sex with me. After months of wrangling and unsuccessful attempts to find a solution, I had ended up feeling sexually frustrated and in need of an outlet. That became focused on a fellow lecturer at the college, a young woman named Margit. We had spent several evenings together at Margit's flat, and one overnight stay. To be honest I was not especially attracted to Margit, but she could be good, outgoing company, she seemed to like me and she enjoyed sex.

At this period I was still lying to Isobel and was not certain whether she knew the truth. I assumed she must as I was careless with clues, but she never said anything.

By four in the afternoon I had reached a decision, and telephoned a family friend named Helen who had sat for Sally on the occasions when Isobel and I wanted to spend an evening out together. I asked her if she would be free that evening and arranged for her to call at seven.

I left the college at five and went straight home. Isobel was ironing some clothes, and Sally – who at this time was six years old – was having her tea.

'Get rid of that as quickly as you can,' I said to Isobel. 'We're going out.'

She was wearing a shapeless blouse and an old skirt. She had no stockings on and was wearing her slippers. Her hair was tied back with an elastic band, though stray wisps fell about her face.

'Going out?' she said. 'We can't leave Sally, and I've got all this to do.'

'Helen's coming round. I've already arranged it. And you can do the rest of that tomorrow.'

'What's to celebrate, Alan?'

'No reason. I just feel like it.'

She gave me an ambivalent look and turned back to her ironing. 'Very amusing.'

'No, I mean it.' I bent down, and pulled the socket of the electric iron from the wall. 'Finish that off, and get ready. I'll put Sally to bed.'

'Are we having a meal? I've bought all the food.'

'We can have it tomorrow.'

'But it's already half-cooked.'

'Put it in the fridge. It'll keep.'

She said quietly, 'Like your mood?'

'What?'

'Nothing.' She bent over her ironing again.

I said, 'Look, Isobel, don't be awkward. I'd like to spend the evening out. If you don't want to go, just say so. I thought you'd like the idea.'

She looked up. 'I do. I'm sorry, Alan. It's just that I wasn't expecting it.'

'You'd like to go then?'

'Of course.'

'How long will it take you to be ready?'

'Not long. I'll have to have a bath and I want to wash my hair.'

'OK.'

She finished what she was doing, then put away the iron and the ironing-board. For a few minutes she moved about the kitchen, dealing with the food she had been cooking.

I switched on the television and watched the news. At this time there was speculation about the date of the coming General Election, and a right-wing Independent Reform MP named John Tregarth had caused a controversy by claiming that Treasury accounts were being falsified. He said he had proof, which he could not produce outside Parliament for fear of arrest. Meanwhile, a number of leaks, apparently sponsored by the government, were acting to incriminate him and lay the blame with the Opposition.

I saw to Sally and washed up the dirty dishes in the sink. I told Sally that Helen was coming over to look after her and that she was to behave. The child promised solemnly that she would, and then became placid and happy. She liked Helen. I went into the bathroom to get my electric razor and Isobel was already in the water. I leaned over and kissed her as she sat in the bath. She responded for a second or two, then pulled away and smiled up at me. It was a curious smile; one whose meaning I could not easily identify. I helped Sally undress, then sat with her downstairs reading to her until Isobel had finished in the bathroom.

I telephoned a restaurant in the West End and asked them to reserve a table for us at eight o'clock. Isobel came down in her dressing-gown while I was speaking to them, looking for her hair dryer. Helen arrived on time at seven, and a few minutes later we took Sally up to her room.

Isobel had brushed her hair down straight and was wearing a pale coloured dress that flattered her figure. She had put on eye make-up and was wearing the necklace I had given her on our first anniversary. She looked beautiful in a way I had not seen for years. As we drove off I told her this.

She said, 'Why are we going out, Alan?'

'I told you. I just felt like it.'

'And suppose *I* hadn't?'

'You obviously do.'

I knew she was not at ease and I realized that to this point I had judged her mood by her behaviour. The cool, beautiful appearance betrayed an inner tautness. As we stopped at a set of traffic lights I looked at her. The drab, almost sexless woman I saw every day was not there. Instead, I glimpsed the Isobel I thought I had married. She took a cigarette from her handbag and lit it.

'You like me dressed up like this, don't you?'

'Yes, of course,' I said.

'And at other times?'

I shrugged. 'You don't always have the opportunity.'

'No. Nor do you often give it to me.' I noticed that she was picking at her nails. She inhaled smoke.

'I wash my hair and put on a clean dress. You wear a different tie. We go to an expensive restaurant.'

'We've done it before. Several times.'

'And how long have we been married? Suddenly it's an event. How long to the next time?'

I said, 'We can do this more often if you like.'

'All right. Let's make it every week. Build it into our routine.'

'You know that's not practical. What would we do about Sally?'

She put her hands to her neck, scooped up her long hair and held it tightly behind her head. I glanced from the traffic to her. She held the cigarette between her lips, her mouth turned down. 'You could employ another drudge.'

For a while we drove on in silence. Isobel finished her cigarette and threw it out of the window.

I said, 'You don't have to wait for me to take you out before you can make yourself look attractive.'

'You've never noticed it at any other times.'

'I have.'

It was true. For a long period after we were first married she had made a conscious effort to retain her looks, even during the pregnancy. I had recognized that, even as the barriers were going up between us.

'I despair of ever pleasing you.'

'You're pleasing me now,' I said. 'You've a small child to look after. I'm out of the house a lot. I don't expect you to dress like this all the time.'

'But you do, Alan. You do. That's the whole trouble.'

I knew we were talking in superficialities. Both of us realized that the subject of Isobel's way of dressing was only peripheral to the real problem. I fostered an image of Isobel as I had first seen her and I was reluctant to let it go. The real reason for my lack of interest in her was something I had never been able to articulate, far less bring out into the open for us to discuss.

We arrived at the restaurant and ate our meal. Neither of us enjoyed it and our conversation was stilted, and punctuated with awkward silences. On the way home afterwards Isobel still said nothing until I stopped the car outside the house.

Then she turned and looked at me, wearing the expression I had seen before, but then she had concealed it with a smile. Now there was no smile.

She said, 'I was just another of your women tonight.'

Two men carried me to the barricade. I had one arm braced around each of their shoulders, and though I tried to put weight on my sprained ankle I found the pain was too severe.

A movable section of the barricade was opened from the far side and they carried me through.

I was confronted by several men. Each carried a rifle. I explained who I was and why I wanted to enter the town. They asked me if I knew anyone in Worthing, or had relatives here. I said no. I did not mention the Afrims, nor that I feared Sally and Isobel were in their hands. I said that I had been separated from my wife and daughter, that I had reason to believe they had been brought here to Worthing and I was trying to find them.

They asked me for their names and they wrote them down. My possessions were searched.

'You're a scruffy sod, aren't you?' one of the younger men said. The other men glanced at him quickly and I thought I detected a quiet warning in the way they did this.

I said, as calmly as I could, 'I've lost my home and all my property. I lived and worked in London until the Africans forced me out. There was nowhere we could go. I've been forced to live off the land for many months. If I could find a bath and some clean clothes I'd gladly use them.'

'That's all right,' one of the others said. He jerked his head to the side and the younger man moved away, glaring at me.

'What did you do before you were displaced?'

'You mean my profession? I was a lecturer at a college, but I lost my job there and had to do manual work for a time.'

'You lived in London?'

'Yes. I said that.'

'Whereabouts in London?'

'Southgate. Do you know it?'

'I've heard of it. Near Barnet, right? It could have been worse. You heard what happened up north when the refugees moved in?'

'I heard some of it. But I've had to live rough. The only information you can get is rumours. Look, are you going to let me in?'

'We might. But we want to know more about you first.'

I was asked several questions. I did not answer them entirely honestly, because I didn't see what business it was of these men, but I was keen to get past them and into the town itself. The questions concerned my involvement with the war, whether I had been attacked by any troops, whether I had initiated sabotage, where my loyalties lay.

I said, 'This is Nationalist territory, isn't it?'

'We're loyal to the crown, if that's what you mean.'

'Isn't it the same thing?'

'Not entirely. There are no troops here. We handle our own affairs.'

'What about the Afrims?'

'There aren't any.' The direct flatness of his tone startled me. 'There were some, but they left. It was only bad decision-making that allowed the situation to get out of hand elsewhere.'

Another man came forward. 'You haven't said what your stand is.'

'Can't you imagine?' I said. 'The Africans took over my home and we ended up on the street. I've had to live like an animal for nearly a year. The bastards have taken my child and my wife. I'm with you. All right?'

'OK. But you said you've come here looking for them. There aren't any Africans here.'

'I thought they were everywhere, especially around the coast.'

'None of them here.'

'I know. You told me.'

'This is Worthing, but you'll find it's the same all along the coast. Certainly as far as Brighton. There have been no Africans here since we kicked the last lot out. If you're looking for them, you won't find them. Understood?'

'You've told me. I've made a mistake. I'm sorry.'

They moved away from me and conferred privately for a minute or two. I took the opportunity to examine a large-scale map which was attached to the side of one of the concrete slabs forming the barricade. This region of the coast was densely populated and although each of the towns had a separate name and identity, in fact their suburbs ran into one another. The part of the town I had been heading for, near Shoreham, was at least another hour's walk from here.

I noticed that the map was marked with a zone outlined in bright green ink. Its northernmost point was just above where the barricade was situated, not far from the beginning of the Downs. It ran down to the east and west until it reached the coast. My objective seemed to be outside the green perimeter.

I tested my ankle and found that it was almost impossible to put weight on it. I began to worry that I had broken a bone in it. Much of the foot was now swollen and I knew that if I removed my shoe I would be unable to get it on again. I needed medical advice, someone to look at it, perhaps bind it up.

The men returned to me.

'Can you walk?' one of them said.

'I don't think so. Is there a doctor here?'

'You'll find one in the town.'

'Then you're letting me in?'

'We are. But a few words of warning. Get some clean clothes and tidy yourself up. This is a respectable town. Don't stay on the streets after dark, find somewhere to live. If you don't, you'll be slung out. The seafront and beach are patrolled every night, so don't think of going down there. And the shops. Don't go around talking about the blacks. That's the main condition of entering the town. You got that?'

I nodded. 'What if I want to leave?'

'Where would you want to go?'

I reminded him that I was looking for Sally and Isobel. This meant I would have to pass through the eastern border towards Shoreham. He told me that I would be able to leave along the coast road.

He indicated that I was to move on. I got to my feet with the greatest difficulty. I had rarely felt pain like this. One of the men went into a house and returned with a walking stick. I was told that I must return it when my ankle had healed. I promised I would, but already I did not mean to.

Slowly, and in tremendous pain, I limped down the road in the direction of the centre of the town. I knew I remained in sight of the men at the barricade for at least another half-hour, because I was having to hobble so slowly. I was shaking with pain. All I wanted to do was collapse, lie on the ground, close my eyes and just give up, but I knew that if I did they would come down the road for me and throw me out again. I struggled on.

*

At the first sound I was awake and moved across the tent to where Sally was lying asleep. Behind me, Isobel stirred.

A few moments later there was a noise outside our tent and the flap was thrust aside. Two men stood there. One held a flashlight whose beam was directed into my eyes and the other was carrying a heavy rifle. The man with the flashlight came into the tent, seized Isobel by her arm and dragged her out of the tent. She was wearing only her bra and pants. She shouted to me to help but the rifle was between me and her. The man with the flashlight moved away and around the other tents I could hear shouting voices and screams. I lay still, my arm around the now-awakened Sally, trying to soothe her. The man with the rifle was still there, pointing the weapon at me without any movement. Outside, I heard three shots, and I became truly frightened. There was a short silence, then came more screams and more shouted orders in some African language I did not understand. Sally was trembling. The barrel of the rifle was right against my head. Though we were in almost complete darkness, I could make out the shape of the man silhouetted against the faint glow of the sky. Seconds later, another man came back into the tent. He was carrying a flashlight. He pushed past the man with the rifle, and outside two more guns fired. My muscles stiffened. The man with the flashlight kicked me twice, trying to push me away from Sally. I clung to her tightly. She screamed. I was struck across the head by a hand, then again. The other man had hold of Sally and tugged her violently. We clung to each other desperately. She was shouting at me to help her. I was incapable of doing more. The man kicked me again, this time in the face. My right arm came free and Sally was pulled from me. I shouted to the man to leave. I said again and again that she was only a child. She screamed. The men stayed silent. I tried to grab the end of the rifle, but it was thrust violently into my neck. I backed away and Sally was dragged struggling through the flap. The man with the rifle came into the tent and squatted over me, the barrel pressing against my skin. I heard its mechanism click, and I braced myself. Nothing happened.

The man with the rifle stayed with me for ten minutes and I lay listening to the movements outside. There were many more aggressive and intimidating shouts but no more shots were fired. I heard women screaming and the sound of a lorry engine starting up and driving away. The man with the rifle didn't move. An uneasy silence fell around our encampment.

There was more movement outside and a voice gave an order. The man with the rifle withdrew from the tent. I heard the soldiers drive away.

I cried.

In addition to the pain from my ankle, I felt increasingly nauseated. My head ached and I was dizzy with the feeling of growing sickness. I was able to take only one step at a time, pausing to recover my strength. I knew that at this slow rate of progress I would not reach even the seafront before nightfall. I took many rests.

Once I was out of sight of the barricade I was in suburban streets which, because of their façade of normality, appeared strange to me. I had spent so long in the world of hedges, barns and ditches. The houses were neat, in good repair, and most of them had cars parked in the road outside or pulled up on to a drive in front. There was traffic: I immediately thought of the phrase 'civilian traffic', as military manoeuvres were more or less all I had seen on the roads for nearly a year. It took a mental effort to realize that this was normal traffic, people going about their ordinary lives.

I saw a middle-aged couple sitting in folding chairs in the garden in front of their house, and they regarded me curiously. I briefly gained a flashing insight into how I must look to them: ragged, unshaven, hair wild, weighed down with plastic bags and camping equipment, leaning painfully on a stick. They said nothing, looked away, almost as if embarrassed by me. I went on past as quickly as I could, my jaw and neck muscles tensing against the pain that every step sent coursing through me.

I came to an intersection with a larger road. Here I saw more traffic and a Worthing Corporation bus. The sun went behind a cloud, then came out again. On the other side of the road was a billboard, advertising a weight-loss preparation. I waited for a gap in the traffic before attempting to cross the road. I managed it with great difficulty, having to pause on the traffic island to get my strength back. When I reached the far side the nausea intensified suddenly and I had to throw up on the ground. I was aware of people staring at me. A small group of children regarded me from a garden, and one of them ran into the house.

As soon as I was able I limped on.

I had no idea where I was or where I was going. Sweat was running down my body, and soon I had to throw up again. I came to a wooden seat on the side of the road and rested there for a few minutes. I felt utterly weakened.

I passed through a shopping area where there were many people moving from one store to another. I was disoriented again by the outward normality of the streets. For many months I had not known any place where there were shops, where it was possible to find goods available for purchase. Most shopping areas I had seen were looted, burnt out or under strict military control.

At the end of the row of shops I halted once again, more or

less unable to walk any further. I had left the barricade about an hour and a half before, which meant that the time now would be around five or six in the evening. I realized how exhausted I was, as well as the other symptoms I was experiencing. I smelt of vomit – there were streaks of it down the front of my jacket. Few of the people in the street came near me. I was obsessed with the thought that I was an offensive spectacle to the people, that if I just stood there indefinitely in the end someone would physically attack me. I backed away into a side street, trembling and shaking. I carried on as long as I could, but I had staggered only a short way from the turning when I fell to the ground for the second time that day. I lay helplessly, trying to get my strength back. In a while, I became aware of voices and people were standing around me. I tried to speak to them, but it was impossible. I was lifted gently away from the ground.

A soft bed. Cool sheets. A body cleaned with a bathful of hot water. A painful leg and foot. A painting of an English thatched cottage on a wall; photographs of smiling people, standing in groups, displayed neatly on a dresser. A row of book-club editions on a shelf. Discomfort in my stomach. Someone else's pyjamas. A doctor winding a bandage around my ankle, telling me to take painkillers. A glass of water at my side. Comforting words. Sleep.

I learned that their names were Mr and Mrs Jeffery. His first name was Charles; hers was Enid. He had been a bank manager before retirement, while she had been a florist. I didn't like to ask them their ages, but they must have been in their middle or late seventies. They were remarkably incurious about me, even though I told them I had come from outside the town. I said nothing of Sally or Isobel.

They told me I could stay as long as I wished, but at least until my ankle was better.

Mrs Jeffery brought me all the food I could eat. Fresh meat, eggs, vegetables, bread, fruit. Chocolate, freshly brewed tea, ground coffee. Apples! At first I registered surprise, saying that I thought food like this was impossible to obtain. She told me that the local shops had regular supplies of groceries and could not understand why I had thought this.

'Food is so expensive though,' she said to me. 'I can hardly keep up with the price rises.'

I asked her why she thought prices had increased.

'It's the times changing. Not like they were when I was younger. Things are complicated now, with those tariffs and these people coming into the country. My mother used to be able to buy bread at a penny a loaf. But there's nothing we can do about it, so I just pay up and try not to think about it.'

'You hear stories these days,' Charles said. 'People fighting for food, that sort of thing. That's what drives up the prices, they claim.'

Enid was marvellous to me. There was nothing that was too much to ask of her. She brought me newspapers and magazines, and Mr Jeffery gave me cigarettes and some Scotch whisky. I read the journals eagerly, hoping they would be able to provide me with some information on the present political scene and what was happening in the civil war.

The newspaper was the *Daily Mail* and was, as Enid told me without any apparent surprise, the only one being published at the moment. Its editorial content was mainly foreign news and photographs, with several pages of gossip about celebrity singers, foreign footballers and film stars. There was no mention anywhere of the war. There were few advertisements and those were mainly for consumer goods. I noticed that there were only twelve pages, that it was printed twice a week and that it was published from an address in Northern France. I passed on none of these observations to the Jefferys. At least it looked like the former newspaper.

The rest and comfort allowed me time to think objectively about the situation I was in. I realized that ever since being thrown out of our home I had been concerned mainly with surviving and with introspection about my personal life, and I had given few thoughts to what our long-term prospects might be or what plans I should make. Lying there in the Jefferys' spare bedroom, or sharing a meal with them down-stairs, gave me much time for reflection. I was still obsessed with the need to find Sally, rescue her from whatever hell she had been thrown into. But the longer I stayed in this pleasant house in a side street in Worthing, warm, comfort-able, dry, clean, not half-starving, regaining my health, the more it seemed I had passed through some kind of emotional portal from one part of my life to another.

The ease of this period lulled me. I was seduced by the homely, familiar comforts, the self-deluding niceness of Charles and Enid Jeffery. Then, as my strength returned, I began to change back, acknowledging how incomplete my life had become, how I had to confront all that and actu-ally take some kind of redeeming action. For too long I had circuited life on the outer rim, before and after the civil war. I began to fret at my inactivity, even though I recognized that it would serve no useful purpose to move until I could walk properly again.

The questions were the same whether or not I was able to find Isobel and Sally. In my unwitting role as refugee I had necessarily been a victim, had played a neutral role. But it seemed to me that it would be impossible for this to continue in the future. I could not stay uncommitted for ever.

From what I had seen of the activities and outlook of the Secessionist forces, it appeared to me that they adopted a more humanitarian attitude to the situation. It was not right to deny the African immigrants an identity or a voice or a place to live. They were here in Britain, largely through no fault of their own, and whatever anyone might feel about that they were here to stay. Protest and fighting must stop, actions should be taken to absorb the refugees into our culture and society. It would need new laws, a new outlook, perhaps years of difficulties with extremist opposition, but in the end an acknowledgement that a healthy society was one that could assimilate other cultures.

On the other hand ...

There was, though, the other hand. It cast a dark shadow on me, and I could not crawl away from it. The extremist actions of the Nationalist side, which stemmed initially from the conservative and repressive policies of the Reform government, appealed to me on a gut level. I could not deny that, could not escape it. It was the African refugees whose brutal invasion of the cities had directly deprived me of everything I once owned. I still seethed with resentment, while I struggled with an inner fear of what that resentment might one day force me to do. I ached to take revenge. I could not suppress the ache, even while I knew it was wrong.

Ultimately, I knew the question depended on my finding Isobel. If she and Sally had not been harmed my instincts would be quieted.

I could not contemplate the consequences of the alternative.

I felt the dilemma was largely of my own making. Had I come to grips with the failures in my life, earlier, in the years before the refugee crisis began, I suspected I would not have reached this state. I had drifted through my adult life in a haze of complacency, shallow motives, indecision, selfishness, self-deluding in a way not entirely dissimilar from what I detected in Charles and Enid Jeffery themselves. I could not defend that, but it meant when the crisis broke around me I was unable to cope with it. On a personal, practical level I could see that whatever future there was for me or my family, it would not be one which we could settle until the larger issues around us were resolved.

On the fourth day at the Jefferys' I was able to get up and move around the house. I had trimmed my beard and Enid had washed and repaired my clothes. As soon as I was mobile I wanted to pursue my search for Isobel and Sally, but my ankle still hurt when I walked. Enid removed the bandage the doctor had placed on my ankle, and we saw that the swelling was going down. She replaced the bandage with another from the family first-aid kit, binding the ankle less tightly, while still supporting it. I helped Charles with light tasks in the garden and spent several hours in conversation with him.

I was continually surprised by the lack of awareness displayed by both him and his wife. When I spoke of the civil war, he referred to it as if it were in another continent. Remembering the injunction given to me by the man at the barricade not to speak of the Afrims, I was cautious about discussing the politics involved. But Charles Jeffery was not interested in them. As far as he was aware, the government was dealing with a difficult social problem and the solution would be found in the end.

Several military aircraft flew over the house during the day, and in the evenings we heard distant explosions. They always sent a chill through me, but none of us mentioned them. It was possible to see the rise of the South Down hills from Charles's garden, and I knew what was happening in the countryside just beyond those gentle, familiar slopes.

The Jefferys had a television set which I watched with them during the evenings. I was fascinated to discover that the service had been restored.

The style of presentation was similar to that which had once been adopted by the BBC, and in fact the station identification was given as 'BBC National South'. The content of the programmes was largely American. There was one short news bulletin in the middle of the evening, which touched on issues local to the south coast towns, making no mention of the civil war. All the other programmes were apparently pre-recorded or imported, and consisted mainly of light entertainment, police procedurals or situation comedies.

I asked the Jefferys if they knew where the programmes were transmitted from. They told me that they were part of a cable system, originating in Brighton. They said most of the towns along the coast, from Dover in the east to Portsmouth in the west, had access to this cable service, and that a second one, based in London, was planned for later in the year.

On the fifth day I felt that my ankle had mended enough to let me move on. The Jefferys pleaded with me to stay, and offered me the use of their spare bedroom whenever I wanted it. In this brief stay, I had grown attached to these pleasant, straightforward people, and in all honesty the temptation to accept was almost irresistible.

I knew, of course, that I could never settle anywhere until I had completed what I had set out to do.

I left them in the afternoon. Enid was in tears, and Charles was stiff with suppressed emotion. I hugged them both, then shook hands. They wished me well, using curiously formal language. I stared at them for a long time, wordless with emotion, feeling only the inadequacy of words or even deeds in the reality of the world that existed outside the bounds of theirs.

I turned away, following their directions through the town centre, looking for the coast road.

There were no difficulties at the barricade. The men who were on guard could not understand why I should ever wish to leave their Worthing, with its buses and Post Office and cable TV and well-stocked shops and the cinema in the High Street. They clearly thought I was mad. I made it plain to them that I genuinely wished to leave. Shrugging their shoulders, they allowed me through. I told them that I might be returning to the town later in the day, but they warned me it would not be as easy to re-enter as it had been to leave.

I walked for two hours through what had been suburban streets. Most of the houses were empty and several had been damaged or destroyed. I saw no civilians. Every shop had been torched.

On several occasions I met small groups of Afrim soldiers. I stepped away, tried to make myself inconspicuous, but they weren't interested in me.

I entered an empty house to eat the beef sandwiches and salad which Enid Jeffery had given me. I drank the flask of tea, and washed it out afterwards, realizing that it might be useful in the future. I then brushed my teeth, combed my hair and straightened my clothes.

I went down to the beach and walked along it until I came to the place where I had found the bungalow with the makings for petrol bombs. Out of curiosity I entered the bungalow and looked for the bombs, but they had been taken by someone else. I expected no different.

I moved on down to the beach. I sat on the pebbles.

Half an hour later a youth walked along the shore and approached me. After our initial wariness of each other he ambled across to me. He stood a short distance away, kept circling me. He told me about a group of British refugees based in the next inhabited town to the east who had commandeered a ship and who were planning to sail to France. He invited me to join them. I asked him if the group were armed and he told me they were.

We spoke for a while about the Afrims and how many there might be in the area. The youth told me that this had once been set up as a garrison town but that their organization was not good. Recently there was a raid by Nationalist forces and the Afrim troops had dispersed. But, he said, they're back and they're everywhere again now.

I told him I had seen some while I walked along the sea road.

'It's the Nationalist army you have to be careful of,' he said. 'If you're not with them, they assume you're against them. They shoot.'

The last traces of the comforting feelings induced by my stay with the Jefferys slipped away. The young man's words, his cynical attitude, his world-weary manner, took me back to my own experiences in the rough. The mixed feelings about the Africans, the sorrow and the pity and the hatred of them, but also the fear of the Nationalists with their vicious intents, the contempt for the ineffectual Secessionists, and the mute anger and frustration induced by the humanitarian aid agencies. I looked down the shingle towards the sea, whose colour at this time of day was turning to a dull silver, with darker streaks. This small British island we lived on, resistant to invasion for so many hundreds of years, a coherent, eccentric, tolerant place, rich in tradition, filled with a relaxed regard for history. The British were welcoming to strangers but also cautious of them and sometimes given to pointed but affectionate mockery after they left, but this time, crucially, they had allowed a massively disruptive refugee incursion almost by default. Tolerance and eccentricity were luxuries of the past, and the British had revealed themselves as congenitally unable to react moderately to an extreme event.

That sea, so calm and silver at low tide, was always a symbol for the British, the image of isolation and difference from the rest of the world, the maritime nation that stood only a short distance away from the continental coast of the largest landmass on the planet. Yet the sea also suggested connectedness with that larger world, because the maritime heritage had taken the British out to the world, for good or ill. Once the British had dominated half of Africa, owned or grabbed a line of huge territorial possessions that ran north–south in an unbroken red swathe on the globes that stood in every British schoolroom. When the British retreated to their island, exhausted by two European wars and in the process giving up on their Empire, the world for a while seemed a better, fairer place without the English colonists. It was the greatest of ironies because the British imperialist impulse had been based on the tacit intention to take the British sense of justice, fairness and opportunity to the world's most unprivileged places. Then came historical happenstance, and the Africans fled their own lands, spread themselves out into the world, went in desperation everywhere to seek a sanctuary, landed on the shores of every continent, but only here, on the quiet offshore island, rich in tradition and relaxed with history, did chaos ensue.

The tide was out, here on the southern British coast, revealing the uncomfortable shingle with its shallow pools, a cooling exposure to the sky before the tide turned and the sea came back. What was revealed at every turn of the tide?

I had walked away from the young man, preoccupied by my thoughts, and stumbled down the shifting shingle bank to where hard sand, still glistening from the tide, spread out towards where the calm wavelets were breaking. Because I had left all my possessions, I went back quickly, scrambling back up the shingle, realizing that I knew nothing of this young man who had wandered by. Everything I still owned was in the bags I carried.

He was sitting there beside my stuff, though, not interested in theft, watching me while I paced about on the wet sand. As I clambered back up towards him, he stood up.

'Have you decided?' he said.

'Decided what?'

'Do you want to join our ship going across to France?'

'I don't think so,' I said. 'I don't know.'

'We're sailing from Shoreham tomorrow. High tide in the evening. We won't be coming back.'

'OK, maybe I'll get there. I've always wanted to visit France.'

'Never been there?'

'Not even when I could.'

He raised his hand in farewell, and began crunching his way along the stony shore in the direction of Worthing.

After a moment I called to him, and he turned.

'Do you know anything about an Afrim brothel?' I said. 'I heard they had opened one for their troops, somewhere around here.'

'Yeah – there was one.'

'What about it? Where is it?'

'It was closed when the garrison moved. But that was only a few days ago. It might still be there, might have opened again.'

'Where?' I said again.

'Not far. Ten minutes' walk. Down there, an old hotel.'

He began describing what he knew, but somehow a churning in my mind made it difficult to hear what he was saying. Mostly white women, he was saying. White women, and teenagers. They were free to leave, if they wanted, but if they tried they were usually shot. Bodies on the beach, he said. Down there by the old hotel. A place with white-painted stucco, standing back from the seafront, slightly raised on a low headland. You can't miss it. You'll smell the place before you see it, all those bodies dumped on the beach.

I was backing away from him while he spoke, while the clangour in my mind tried to deafen me to what he was saying. I was backing off, in the direction of the hotel.

I stayed on the beach, returning down the shingle ramp to the damp plain of tide-exposed coarse sand. When I was closer to the sea I saw that far from being the clean expanse I had imagined, the water was dirty and spoiled. Those darker streaks were something that had spilled into the sea, oil perhaps, or something worse. There was a pervading smell of oil, or diesel fuel. I could see traces of fuel residue on the sand, bright colours glowing and shifting prismatically. There were also harder mounds of crude oil, spillage dumped ashore by the waves and left to coagulate in the sand.

I walked slowly in the direction that the youth had indicated the old hotel would be found. Within five minutes I had seen it. I recognized it from his description, because although in earlier times it had been a typical Victorian English seaside hotel, there were now several Afrim flags flying on the roof and the white walls had been daubed with slogans. I headed up from the beach towards it, but when I was not far away I realized there were many Africans hanging around outside.

I could smell the stench the youth had described.

Evening was coming on. A wind had risen from the direction of the sea, helping to disperse the terrible stink a little, but bringing in fresh drafts of the smell of oil spillage.

I was tired, and my ankle was aching. I returned to the beach. I sat down on the shingle and looked out at the sea.

Here there was much more crude oil floating in slicks on the surface of the sea, and in many places the beach was covered in thick black sludge.

The silence appalled me.

There were no seabirds, and the oily waves that broke on the shore were sluggish and without foam. The tide was slowly flowing in. Out to sea there was a large warship, but I couldn't see it clearly enough to recognize what type of ship it was, or whose navy it belonged to. I wondered what it was doing out there, stationary in the sea, unthreatened by any other boat, just off the English coast. One of its turrets had been turned so that its guns pointed towards the land.

I discovered where the bodies were being left when unexpectedly I saw a squad of Afrim soldiers moving down the beach. They were carrying or dragging several large objects, which they dumped without ceremony on the lower part of the shingle. They then returned towards the building.

I stood up.

As I walked across to where the men had been my feet were sucked by a thick layer of oil on the shingle. The bodies were not easy to see and had I not been looking for them I might easily have mistaken them for more large chunks of congealed crude oil. They were black and there were twenty-two of them. They were naked, and they were all female. The blackness of the skin was not that of natural pigmentation or of oil, but of paint or pitch.

I moved amongst them, covering my mouth and nose with my sleeve, trying to filter out the appalling stink of decomposing flesh. Eventually I found two bodies thrown together on to the beach, curled one on top of the other. I recognized Isobel by her hair. I recognized Sally by her face.

I noticed no reaction in me. I felt immune to everything. I was at last cut off from my feelings, a ghoul, a vestige of myself. I could not stay by the bodies, because the fouled air was almost impossible to breathe. I backed off, walked down to where the sea began, walked back, walked away, avoided the bodies, returned, stared again at the bodies, stood by the waves and looked at the warship, went back, kicking against the sand, then down the beach, then back, endlessly round, flailing mentally and physically for a sense of direction. Later, I felt sadness, and later than that a terrible combination of forlorn fear and uncontrollable hatred.

I stayed on the beach that night, upwind of the bodies. I lay there shivering as the tide came in, touched the bodies without removing them, and then went out again. The sea frightened me with its unstoppable quality, the way it could be tainted but not altered, that it would come in and go out as it had to. It was a cold, moonless night. I was not thinking, I was not able to think. I stayed alive. All I could feel was the engagement, at last, of emotion.

In the early morning I went into the town, murdered a young African and stole his rifle, and by the afternoon I was again in the countryside.